Joyce Stranger's latest novel will delight
her readers. Another heart-warming,
enthralling story of people and
animals, such as only she can create.

Khazan left Ireland as a champion, and
was castaway in Cornwall to be reborn
as 'Blaze', Debbie Trelawney's horse.
The magnificent thorough-bred and
the frail young girl formed a wonderful
bond which could never be severed.
He was a wonder horse – a horse who
could somehow change people's lives;
a horse who aroused fierce pride and
loyalty; a horse of unique character who
remained an enigma all his life.

Also by Joyce Stranger

and published by Corgi Books

Joyce Stranger

KHAZAN

CORGI BOOKS

KHAZAN

A CORGI BOOK 0 552 11014 0

Originally published in Great Britain by
COLLINS & HARVILL PRESS

PRINTING HISTORY
Collins & Harvill edition published 1977
Corgi edition published 1979
Corgi edition reissued 1983

This book is set in 10-10½ pt Pilgrim

Corgi Books are published by Transworld Publishers Ltd.,
Century House, 61-63 Uxbridge Road,
Ealing, London, W5 5SA
Made and printed in Great Britain by
Hunt Barnard Printing Ltd., Aylesbury, Bucks.

To Nick's Jean and to Andrew's Vivienne
who are now part of our family — with my love

Acknowledgements

My thanks are due to Peter Gorvin for his help and the loan of vital books on the racing scene – I wish his racehorse luck in her first season and those to come.

And also particularly to David Nicholson, who gave me time in a very busy day, and allowed me to look around the stables, talk to the lads and see the horses, at his training establishment at Stowe-on-the-Wold.

The story is based very freely on the legend of Moifaa, a New Zealand horse who was supposed to have come from the sea; who won the Grand National in 1904, and was then bought by King Edward VII. Both horses came from the sea, but there is no other resemblance.

All people, places and characters are fictitious.

Chapter One

Joe Garnery huddled into his overcoat. It had been a rough passage, and he had been sick all the way, cursing the treacherous sea; cursing Matt Keene, his partner, who had persuaded him to travel to Ireland to some benighted farm that no one had ever heard of, to look at a horse that just might prove a good one.

It was insane; the whole thing was absurd. It had been a race-course rumour that sent him off on this crazy chase, with the wind blowing half a gale, though luckily they had landed before it got worse. The thought of the passage home dominated every other thought in his mind. He hadn't been able to eat since he landed, the car he had hired was a horror, with a steering-column gear change that slipped out in second. And the journey was hilly.

Now he was standing in an almost derelict yard, thinking of the stud farm at home, with its rolling acres and well-fenced paddocks and beautiful mares. And then the other worry he had had all day flared into life as he thought of Fantasia, their best mare and his especial favourite and her foal that was due any day now. If she foaled when he was away, anything might happen. He didn't trust anyone else to foal his mares. He should never have agreed to leave home. But he could bargain. Matt always overpaid.

'It's a great horse,' Paddy Rafferty said, standing beside him. Paddy had managed this tiny stud for most of his life. Dan Flanagan, who owned it, was very young when his father died, and Paddy had taken over until the boy was old enough to manage for himself. By then Paddy was as much an institution as was Joe in the stud back home.

Joe knew about horses. And race-course rumours. They were both mad – he and Matt should have known better. It would be an old nag with a broken wind; it would never have run a race in its life, or if it had, and had won, there would only have been two runners. Paddy had kissed the Blarney Stone and you couldn't believe a word he said. Joe wished he were safe in England, in his bed. He still felt as sick as a cat that had been fool enough to eat a shrew.

He didn't even look at the horse as Dan led it round the corner. Instead, he straightened a leaning fence post and then wished he hadn't as Dan's lips tightened. He knew the place was ramshackle, but there wasn't any time and there wasn't any help and there wasn't any money. If there had been, he wouldn't be selling this horse now.

Dan led the horse forward into the yard. The soft muzzle nosed against his cheek and he felt again the hard knot of misery in his stomach. He looked at Paddy who was standing, expressionless, avoiding Dan's eyes.

'This is Khazan,' Dan said, as if he were introducing an emperor.

Joe lifted his head. He'd look over the beast for decency's sake and then go home. He was dying and no one cared. He pulled his coat closer around him and then looked at the horse.

He immediately closed his eyes, terrified lest they betray him. The horse was magnificent. He hadn't seen a horse like that for over forty years. His memory went back to himself standing with his father at the rails at the edge of the race-course as the most wonderful horse in all history raced home for the hundredth time, far ahead of the field. The fabulous Golden Miller.

This was his reincarnation. The wide head; the intelligent eyes; the strong legs. The powerful chest. Joe forgot his sea-sickness. He forgot he was cold and felt ill and tired and old. He forgot about Fantasia, his English beauty. They had to have that horse. On it Matt could gallop to victory and achieve the goal he had longed for ever since he could ride. Joe had a sudden vision of his partner at ten years old, wickedly determined, never to be deterred from any course he had set his heart on, declaring, 'One day I'll win the Grand National. You'll all see.' Matt hadn't even owned a horse then. He stole rides on Joe's horses. And because of that he and Joe had got together when Matt inherited his father's immense wealth, which came from selling scrap metal during the last war.

10

The old man hadn't thought much of breeding race-horses. But it had paid off; it was still paying off, though not so well. In spite of their successes, breeding flat winners, Matt had never forgotten his dreams. He had ridden once in the National on a horse they thought had quality, but he had fallen at Beecher's Brook. And that had been the end of it all for many years.

Until a rumour came on the grapevine and Joe made a journey and came face to face with a miracle.

'Well?' Dan said impatiently and Joe knew that to criticise this horse would be as bad as criticising a woman's first child. And he had to do it, or the price would soar sky high.

'It's not bad,' he said grudgingly, as if the words were dragged from him. He pulled his greatcoat tighter and shivered. 'You have mortal cold weather over here.'

Dan glared at him. He adjusted the horse's rug, and Khazan dipped his head and dropped his tongue into the man's hand. Dan squeezed, and for some moments hoped that Joe would go away, and they could keep the animal. Misery tightened his face. It was as bad as parting with a member of the family. They'd grown up together. He'd helped to bring the foal into the world; had gentled him and schooled him and jumped him daily.

Every day he felt the surging power beneath him, and knew the exhilaration of cantering wildly over the fields, giving the horse his head.

They were a familiar sight to everyone for miles around. Dan and Zan. One day they'd make history. But one day had never come, and unless they could get a good price for this horse, the place would have to be sold up. There were feed bills to pay and vet bills and shoeing bills.

Joe looked at the horse again. This was an aristocrat. The glorious coat gleamed like sunlight itself. The horse was made for running and for jumping; that deep chest would hold a massive heart and great lungs that could stand the strain of a real race. Khazan was a racing machine, built for power. He was most impressive, but Joe was too old a hand to give anything away. Many a stable lad regretted taking him on at poker.

'He's the best horse we ever bred,' Dan said, passion in his voice. 'He's a king. You won't find another horse like him anywhere this side of the Atlantic. He's as good as all the great names rolled into one. He's descended from a daughter of Golden Miller's dam; and you know what the Miller was like.'

So his eyes hadn't misled him. Golden Miller in the 1930s. Winning race after race after race. Joe had been a young man then, a frequent attender at as many meetings as he could manage, entering the odd horse of his own, longing for the day when he would own a beast that could pick up the money as the Miller had picked it up. The Cheltenham Gold Cup, five years running. The Grand National. You name it, the Miller won it. He'd been a famous horse and was now a legend.

If you believed in reincarnation then this was it. Khazan. It was a name that would look well on the records. It was a name that suited the horse. It was a name destined for headlines. But Joe wasn't giving anything away. He walked round the animal, his eyes critical.

Dan removed the rug.

Khazan watched the little man curiously. The great chestnut knew this was a man he could trust; a man who knew about horses. He waited passively, used to his routine, used to being admired. He knew, from the hand that touched his withers, that this man did admire him. He stood proudly, showing off.

Paddy's eyes narrowed. He knew that reaction well. The stable manager might have been a horse himself. He could read their minds and this horse had responded as if to spoken admiration. Dan hadn't noticed. It took years to interpret those movements. They could push Joe up; but not too far. He wasn't a fool. And they needed the money, honest to God, how they needed the money. Paddy made a small and hasty prayer. The horses were all his life and without them there would be no future, for him or for Dan.

Joe shivered.

'Come in and have a drink and a bite,' Paddy said.

'I'm not sure about eating. It was a rough passage.'

'We've a great whisky indoors. It was a present from a man who left a horse here for a few weeks while he had his stable rebuilt,' Paddy said. 'It lies sweetly on the tongue, and it will settle your stomach for you. You might even be able to face Bridgie's cooking after it. Dan's mother's in her bed with a migraine, or you'd have a meal for a prince.'

Dan led the horse off. Paddy was talking too much. Joe wasn't interested. He was a fool who didn't know good breeding when he saw it, but Dan had to be polite. Had to play the host and pour the drinks, with anger choking him. Not knowing if the anger was because he hadn't sold the horse, or because he had to sell the horse. Either way his temper was rising. He hated Joe, who had come to see the horse and then failed to admire him.

Joe and Paddy were reminiscing about the Miller. It was before Dan's time, as far away in his mind as the First World War and as remote, except that blood always told, and you bred on, and on, using all the great mares and stallions, until one day you pulled it off, and got a marvel. That last mating had been Paddy's idea; and the horse was brilliant, no mistake.

'The Miller was one of my heroes,' Joe said. He masticated the stringy meat and chewed on the tasteless dumplings, but the whisky had shifted the nausea and the thought of the horse had warmed him. He would play it cool, but he would phone Matt before the day was out. 'I had pin-ups of him all over my room. And I've a picture of him now in my sitting-room. A head study. Nothing born will ever touch him. He was a one-off; a miracle. You'll not see his kind again.'

'It's out there in my stable,' Dan said. 'And worth a fortune to the man who buys him.'

'Not today,' Joe said. 'A few years ago maybe when good stock fetched a good price. But money's scarce now, wages are high and look at the cost of feed. That fellow will eat his head off for months before he's any good to us. Have you ever raced him?'

'I've raced him over hurdles. He won his fourth race.'

'What distance?'

'Two miles,' Dan said. 'We've no time for much racing here. There's only the two of us, and we've six mares. I didn't mean to keep that horse; but somehow, we couldn't part with him. We don't want him to go now, but I haven't time to ride and train him. The mares are our livelihood.'

Joe drank the execrable coffee, and walked out into the yard. The wind was still rising.

'Gales all round the British Isles,' Dan said. 'I heard a forecast just before you arrived. When are you returning?'

'Not for a couple of days, thank God,' Joe said. 'I've other horses to see. I'll come back to you. Maybe tomorrow. It depends on the horse I'm looking at this afternoon. Another world-beater, if his owner is to be believed. I might just take your horse on too. Matt wants a hunter, and he likes spirit. But as for racing . . . forget it. That horse hasn't got it in him. And he's not halfway fit.'

He drove out of the yard. He turned his head as he reached the lane and looked back. Paddy and Dan were arguing, and the horse was standing by the paddock gate, posed as if for a picture. Dear heaven, what a horse. What a horse!

Joe whistled as he drove. He'd never imagined there was a horse like it alive today. It was a jewel of a creature; a prize beyond imagining. It would walk every race they entered it for. It would win the National and Matt would be nine miles high. And the prize money would be useful, too. However wealthy you were there was never enough to do all that was necessary for the future of the place.

Dan was furious.

'The man's a prize idiot,' he said angrily. 'He doesn't know a good horse from a rag and bone man's nag.'

'He knows, all right,' Paddy said. 'He put a hand on Zan, and the horse knew. He stood there, proud, to be admired, every inch of him telling me that he'd just been handled by a man who worshipped him. Garnery's an old hand at this game, but he craves that horse.'

'Are you sure?' Dan asked.

'Honest to God, as sure as I'm standing here,' Paddy said. 'But he'll argue every inch of the way. We'll get a fair price, but he'll not be taken for a ride.'

'I'd no intention of taking him for a ride,' Dan said.

Paddy laughed. 'He could afford it, but we'll not get away with it,' he said. 'You're too soft, lad. We've got a living to make.'

'And I wish to God we hadn't,' Dan said.

That evening he walked over to fetch Khazan from the

paddock. If he had to drop his price, he'd drop it for Joe. The horse would be well treated. Joe was a man he could trust. Paddy would be right about that. Paddy always was. All the same . . . He patted the arched neck, before leading the horse into his stable for the night and bedding him down.

'It's a bleak bitter world, old lad,' he said, as he bolted the lower door. 'But you'll never understand.'

The horse whinnied, as Dan began to close the top half door. He often answered when they spoke. Paddy came over with a carrot in his hand.

'Mustn't forget the routine,' he said, as he reopened the door, and went inside. He stood for a long time in the gloom, wishing with all his heart they could keep Khazan.

Joe drove thirty miles before he spoke to Matt. The line was bad, and there was a whistling wind blowing through a broken pane in the telephone kiosk. Matt sounded faint and far away.

'Is the horse as good as they say?' he asked.

'It's a hundred times better,' Joe answered, and Matt chuckled.

'If you say so. Get it, and go to the limit. OK?'

'OK,' Joe said. He hated the phone. He also hated the wind. 'Is it blowing a gale back home?'

'The river field's flooded and it's black as the pit,' Matt said. 'We're in for a bad night.'

'Watch out for Fan,' Joe said. 'That foal's due very soon. Time she was brought in to the foaling stable. Keep someone with her every second.'

'You buy that horse, and I'll attend to Fan. I'm not ten years old still, Joe,' Matt said. 'She'll be as well looked after as if you were here. Don't worry.'

The line went dead.

It wasn't worth trying to reconnect. Joe went out into a gathering storm. Fantasia hated wind. It made her as edgy as a mother with a newborn child. And Donald, his second in command, had very little experience. And Sally Keene had had a major operation twelve weeks ago and wasn't fit enough to help. He wished she were. She was a farmer's daughter and had a way of her own with the horses. But she had lost a child and then had to have surgery because of a growth and she was as depressed and unhappy as a mare without the foal she had been carrying for eleven months. Females were all the same, beast or human, though they didn't know it.

Joe went to his bed and dreamed of a horse that he led through a crowd that roared with delight, and then, as he turned to unsaddle it, it turned into his employer's wife, standing, looking up at him, saying, 'It's not fair, Joe. It's not fair.' He woke, to doze again uneasily, aware of a wind that tore through the trees and screamed round the corners and flung the nearby sea against the rocks in ever-increasing fury.

Chapter Two

The rainfall over the last five days was the highest recorded for nearly a century. Nobody needed telling that as the stable lads ploughed through the muddy fields, bringing in the horses from the river field.

The field where the practice jumps were rigged for Matthew Keene's hobby horses, on which he rode as an amateur in steeplechases, was under an inch of water. Luckily the stables were on higher ground and the big house was higher still, brooding above the scattered cottages of Cantring under the Hill.

Life had altered very little in the village since the manor house was built in Elizabethan days. Most of the cottages had been added when Queen Victoria was in her cradle. The villagers farmed, or worked in the local pubs or shops. They worked at the big house, but Matthew was a newcomer, arriving only sixteen years ago, using the lodge for his partner's house, and the manor for his own.

His wife was an even more recent arrival, and at first the villagers had been deeply suspicious. She was so much younger than he, and so elegant. But they discovered her father was a Herefordshire farmer, and she herself was passionate about horses. She could talk to them of crops and farm beasts, and wasn't even afraid of the big bull at Sam Walker's, that many men avoided. She rubbed his nose and laughed at his tantrums and the enormous Hereford almost purred to her. The horses adored her. She was a bit of all right, was Mrs Keene.

The villagers had been genuinely sorry when her baby died at birth and they were shocked to hear she had a growth that necessitated a major operation, and no more children. The house had been filled with the flowers they sent to her. They had also made baby clothes. Those she had given to the district nurse. She had closed the door on the freshly-furnished nursery. One day she would turn it into an office for Matt. But not yet.

She sat by the window, watching the lowering sky.

Matthew prowled around the place, worrying. He checked the horses, and the stables, and the mares; he checked Fantasia, who was edgy, and he checked Nayina, one of the yearlings, who stood in her stall, ears flat, eyes wild, panic imminent. He sent one of the lads to sit with her. It would leave them short staffed but it couldn't be helped.

'I shouldn't have sent Joe off; not with Fan due to foal,' he said irritably, coming in for the coffee and sandwiches that his aunt had prepared. Myra Keene had looked after the house ever since Sally became ill. After three and a half months, she felt like an institution. She handed a cup of coffee to Sally and frowned out of the window at the now torrential rain.

'No use being wise by hindsight. The weather's unusual,' she said.

'Fat lot of help that is,' Matt said angrily. He set his lips, and walked over to the window again. Myra moved one of the ornate tables out of the way, wishing for the hundredth time that her nephew liked modern furniture, instead of cluttering the place with heavy antiques that were a nightmare to look after, as they marked so easily.

'Looks like a coffee and sandwich night,' she said briskly, covering an uneasy silence. Sally sat staring into the darkness as if it might bring back her lost hopes.

The wind shrieked round the corners of the house. There

was a whine from behind the high-winged Queen Anne arm-chair in the corner. Sheikh, Sally's golden retriever, crept out and came to her knee and laid his head on it, his eyes miserable.

Matthew looked down at the dog irritably.

'That brute ought to be outside, where he belongs.'

'He's terrified of the wind,' Sally said. 'He'd only howl and upset the mares.'

Sheikh curled up, making himself as small as possible, as if that might help him to become invisible. Matt had little time for the dog. He preferred horses, and could not see why his wife had a soft spot for all small creatures as well as large.

The telephone made all of them jump.

Sally listened to the wind as Matthew answered. This was no ordinary wind. It was a malign beast, increasing moment by moment in force, hurling the trees around the sky, rend-ing tiles from the roof; screaming in the stable yard.

'Trouble,' Matthew said. 'You'd better go to bed. I'll be busy all night.'

'Let me help.' Sally felt useless. She hated not being involved. She was part of the place, which meant as much to her as to Matt; her heart was with the mares and the newborn foals; and she loved to walk the yearlings.

'You're not halfway fit.' Matthew turned towards her, his large body made even larger by the sheepskin coat he had just put on. 'It's no night for passengers.'

He slammed the door, and the dog moved to the hearth-rug, his eyes on the cuckoo clock. The bird leaped out of its hiding place, shouted CUCKOO nine times, and rushed in. The tiny door shut again. Gratified, certain the performance was meant for his entertainment, the dog beat his tail on the rug, moved to lean against his mistress's foot and fell asleep, confident that she could keep at bay the devils that rode through the night, threatening him when he was in the yard, savaging his fur with their terrifying invisible chilly fingers.

'Lucky dog,' Sally said. 'Myra, if I don't get back to work I'll end up in a nuthouse. I need to be occupied, not treated like a lilywhite maid that's going to die any minute. I'm beginning to wake in the night and wonder if you all know something that I don't. That growth wasn't malignant, was it?'

'No, I promise you. It was big, and it grew with the baby; that's why he died,' Myra said, not believing in hiding the truth, and well aware that if she put the point brutally, her niece was likely to believe her on the major issue. 'You only need time; you can't expect to burst into rude health in three months after a packet like that.'

'I feel I've let Matt down,' Sally said. She bent to stroke the dog so that Myra shouldn't see her face. 'He's dynastically minded; a real Victorian *paterfamilias*. That's why he's bought all this furniture; making a stately home for his sons. And now he won't have any.'

'Matt's lived long enough to know life doesn't run on oiled wheels all the time,' Myra said. 'He's bothered about the storm just now; and I think he's having to economise too. He hasn't replaced either of the men who left; and he's selling two of the mares. He says they're non-doers. But he usually retires his mares; he's as soft as you are under all that gruff no-nonsense attitude.'

'I suppose I'm hypersensitive,' Sally said. 'I never thought it would happen to me. I've always thought I could take things. It's time I began to get out and about. I'll have, some time, to face my sisters and their children. Linda has two now; and Janet's little boy must be nearly a year old. I can't go through life full of regrets. But I haven't got used to it.'

She walked impatiently to the window and lifted the curtain.

Lightning scythed the sky.

There was a scream from the stable yard.

Both women ran.

Out into the pouring rain, with the wind catching at their throats, battering their way against a tangible force that was flinging a dustbin lid along in the distance, bowling it like a hoop. A tree uprooted itself, falling slowly, toppling so that its branches lay in the yard, pushing down the fence as it fell.

There were lights in the stable, and voices shouting, and somewhere a door was hammering against the stable side in the wind. Horses neighed. There was the panic thrash of hooves against a partition.

Matt raced into the yard, his shirt bloodstained.

'Matt, are you all right?' Sally had to yell the words as she raced towards him.

She slipped into the office beside the foaling stable. Matt followed her, breathing heavily. Myra shut the door. The wind was held at bay.

'What's wrong?'

'It's not me. It's Donald. One of the mares panicked and kicked him. He's smashed his arm. We need help and the telephone lines have just come down. He ought to get to the hospital. I can't even ring Greene to come and drive. He lives too far away for a lad to walk over. There's a tree down blocking the main road. I don't want anyone out on a horse. It's far too wild tonight.'

'I can take Don to hospital,' Myra said. 'If he's able to walk, it might be wiser to get him there right away. I can drive the estate car. He can lie in the back, with rugs over him. Is there a man free to come with us? I may need help with him, and I can't look after him and drive. I know all the back roads. I've driven over them daily since I arrived.'

'I could come,' Sally said.

'I want one of you here,' Matt said. 'We'll need coffee and sandwiches during the night. No one's going to bed. There's pandemonium out there and worse to come. The weather forecast is appalling, with hurricane force winds. Larry Welsh is with Donald now. He can drive and you can sit in the back and make sure Don's as comfortable as possible.'

Myra went to fetch a coat and blankets, while Matt went off to find Larry and sent him for the car. Sally returned to the house for hot tea, and came back with a tray. Sheikh followed her into the office. Donald was leaning against the table, his face drawn, a white towel, already stained with blood, holding the injured arm against him.

'Is the mare OK?' he asked, as Matt came back into the room.

'She's quiet at the moment. We're in for a bad night,' Matt repeated, anxiety dominating him. 'You sure you're fit to travel? Might be better to get to bed here and wait till morning.'

'He needs attention now,' Myra said. She was wearing a

short fur coat over her slacks. She waited while Donald finished the tea and helped the man to the car, which was now in the yard.

Sally made herself a cup of coffee, and listened to the wind.

'I'd better help out there,' she said.

'And get an arm smashed too? That would be very useful,' Matt said. 'Panicking horses are not a woman's job. Damn that telephone. It's as useless as Joe is in Ireland.'

Sally glanced into the foaling stable through the inspection panel in the office door. A mare was standing deep in straw. She pawed the ground uneasily.

'Is that Fantasia? She's not due till next week, is she?'

'Anything can happen on a night like this,' Matt said. He opened the outer door. The wind tore it from his hands, gusting across the yard. There was a crash of glass.

'Dear God, what was that?' Matt ran. Sally was about to follow him, when she glanced again at the mare. She was stamping in the straw, her head tossing, her eyes wild. She whinnied shrilly.

Sally walked quietly into the foaling room. Fantasia was their best mare, and also one of their favourites. This was her third foal, and nothing should go wrong. But something was wrong. Sally was sure of that; as sure as if she could see inside the mare. In a moment all her own anxieties were forgotten as she stroked the creamy head. Anguished brown eyes stared at her.

She couldn't leave the mare and fetch Matt. Anything might happen in her absence. The useless telephone mocked her. The vet was ten miles away. They needed the vet. Or did they? She had helped at tricky calvings when her parents' farm was isolated by snow. She knew what could be done and what couldn't be done, and maybe she could do something here. Joe always managed the foaling. Matt hated birth. He was a surprisingly squeamish man. Donald's blood would have upset him already.

Matt reappeared at the door, looking for his sheepskin coat.

'The end stable's blown over,' he said. 'One of the horses is trapped. It's going to take hours to sort out. I'm moving the Land-Rovers out there to use the headlights. All the devils in hell are loose tonight. And we're short of men. Can you manage here? Is the mare all right?'

She wasn't all right but what was the use of saying so now? Sally nodded her head, as she stroked the soft neck. They needed help; of that she was becoming increasingly sure. If only she could have rung the vet; he could have told her what to look for; and what to do. The mare was plunging, agonised, her eyes staring at nothing. Sally moved out of the way of the kicking hooves, and then moved back again, her hand soothing.

She began to lead the mare around the box. Walking would help her. It might even distract her. Luckily Fan was used to the foaling box. There had been another mare there until the day before. She was late and Fan was early; nothing ever went according to plan. Joe liked the mares to settle in three weeks before the birth. They hated changes in routine.

The wind tore above them, and the mare reared.

Sally gentled her, a soft voice and a soft hand on her neck; quite suddenly, she was almost enjoying herself, feeling useful again, being needed, after weeks when she had lived in a fog of pain and misery, scarcely knowing what was going on in the world. She was aware of rain drumming on the roof, of a shout from outside, and the stamping hooves of another horse, apparently careering round the yard. They were background noises; all her concentration was on the mare herself, and on the fact that something was wrong with the presentation of the foal.

The mare dropped to the straw, panting.

Wind ripped a corner from the roof. It flapped eerily against the window. The mare struggled to her feet again, but Sally was ready for her.

'It's all right, old girl. It's all right. Let's get on with the job, shall we? Never mind the noises outside.'

The speeding runaway crashed against the office door. Then there was silence, except for the din of the gale. Sally hoped no one had been hurt and no horse had been hurt.

One of the lads, a new man that she didn't know, came into the office. 'I'm to brew more coffee, Mrs Keene. Do you want some?'

'Please,' she said, closing the foaling room behind her,

not wishing to disturb the mare by talking to a stranger. 'There are sandwiches on the table; there ought to be enough. We seemed to be making them for ever.'

'Mr Keene said to ask if the mare's all right.'

'I think so,' Sally said, her fingers crossed behind her back. The man looked at her admiringly; her creamy cheeks were flushed and her black hair had escaped from its restraining chignon, lying loose on her shoulders. The dark blue shirt suited her perfectly, and she was almost as small as he. He had been apprenticed as a jockey but he had never made the grade. He couldn't bear to be away from horses.

'What happened out there?' Sally asked.

'The end of the stable blew away and a mare was trapped. We got the wood off her and she panicked. Mr Keene managed to catch her. He's a way with horses. Reminds me of my old grandad. He was a whisperer.'

'So was mine,' Sally said, suddenly remembering Gramp and the way he managed the big Shires, able to do anything with them. He always swore his father had been a horse thief. She never knew if he were pulling her leg or not. It was strange how often the smallest people were marvellous with the biggest animals.

Sally returned to the office, to look at Joe's veterinary books on mares and their foals. Somewhere there might be a clue as to what was wrong. The mare was straining, but nothing happened. She arched her back and lifted her tail, eyes wide and alarmed, and Sally went in again to coax and soothe. Perhaps a small feed might help to steady Fantasia.

There were sounds from outside where the men struggled against the wind. Sheikh was curled in a corner of the office, between the desk and the wall, where he felt safe. He knew better than to try to follow her into the foaling room. Dogs were not allowed in any stable which contained a horse. They might well get kicked and badly hurt. He sighed sleepily and tucked his nose tightly under his tail. So long as Sally was near, he was content.

The mare settled momentarily. This could go on all night. The wind screeched and rustled the straw, and Sally fetched a technical book and a stool and sat in a corner of the foaling room, ready to move fast if need be. Someone ran into the office, opened a drawer, and glanced through the inspection window.

'Everything OK?' he shouted, his voice distorted by the need to drown the wind.

Sally lifted her hand, thumb up. A sudden yell would alarm the mare. She was used to external noises, but just now she needed absolute quiet. The window rattled and again the loose strip of roofing felt flapped uncannily. The mare reared, fore hooves flailing.

When she was quiet again Sally went outside. The wind took her breath away, but she was able to grab the loose felt and tear it down. Sally had forgotten that she had been ill. She had slipped back to her life on the farm, to Gramps standing beside her, saying, 'Gently does it, girl. Absolute confidence. Don't let the animal sense you're afraid or nervous; that will cause even more trouble. You are the human; it's up to you, all the time. Easy does it. Easy does it.'

There was a cupboard in the office. Sally found Joe's antiseptic lubricant. She also found his clean overalls and put them on, rolling up the sleeves as high as they would go, and covering her arms in the slimy cream.

Not so easy to stand behind the mare with no one to hold her head. There was always danger from those flying hooves and Fan might well whip round and lash out in panic. That could mean a multitude of choices of unpleasant injury.

'Gently, girl. Softly now. Easy, easy, easy.'

Her voice slipped unconsciously into her grandfather's whispering hiss. Ssssss. Ssssss. Her hand explored the passage under the tail. The foal was near to birth. The bag had already burst and he should be out any minute. Or she. But something was stopping further progress. There was a lump in front of the head, barring the way. She tried to remember. Of course she remembered the picture in the book, showing that the foal should lie with his hooves just in front of his nose, both legs almost in a diving position. Then he could slide free easily and quickly.

There was only one hoof.

So the other leg was doubled back and that was the

trouble. It might be an impossible doubling, needing ropes, and she couldn't manage alone. If she were lucky it was only slightly out of position. She could feel farther back now, feeling in the dark, feeling the living animal, moving against her seeking fingers.

And there was the other hoof. Only a little out of position. But if the mare moved suddenly . . . or there came a sudden gust of wind . . . or one of the men came into the office and startled her . . . she couldn't rely on absolute stillness, but the mare had to co-operate. Sssssss. Sssssss. Total concentration, moving the fragile leg, straightening it inch by inch, until at last it was in position.

Both hooves now lay parallel and the foal's head was almost out of the birth passage.

The mare arched her back and spun round, and Sally moved swiftly. The foal slid free, into her waiting hands, and she lowered it to the straw. It was covered in the birth membrane, and she had everything ready to hand. She had remembered it all; once she had wanted to be a vet, finding total satisfaction in helping a new young creature into the world, but she had never before managed a birth quite on her own.

She cleared the membrane from the foal. It breathed shallowly and then sneezed. The mare had come forward to nose it, recognising it as hers. And then Sally realised it was a filly foal; another future mother for the stud, perhaps a mare she could keep for her own, could rear as her own, could use to replace the awful gap left now she could not have a child of her own.

She knelt, holding the tiny head to the udder, while the mare licked at her offspring, deep contentment in her eyes. Pain had gone and this was satisfaction. Sally felt the slender body move against her. The baby had accepted her as well as its mother, and its wide blue eyes stared up at both of them.

There was a lot to do. The stable to clean and the mare to clean, and they couldn't be left alone for a long while yet. The mare needed food. The struggle had exhausted her. Sally put the foal down in the straw, and the mare dropped beside it, licking at the damp coat. They could be left while she prepared the oatmeal gruel and salt that

Joe always gave to his mares after foaling. Everything was ready. Joe was a meticulous man; nothing was missing.

She was conscious of wind and rain again; and conscious of feeling extremely tired. She was aware too of a deep satisfaction, such as she had not experienced for a long time. She finished mixing the feed, and poured it from the saucepan into a metal bowl. It would need to cool a little. She glanced through the inspection panel. The mare lay with the foal cuddled close against her, her eyes dreamy. The small head lifted, the ears pricked, as the office door opened and Matt came in.

'We've got the wood off the mare,' he said. 'Luckily, apart from terror, she isn't harmed. It fell across her, balanced on two joists. We were very lucky . . . I suppose that mare's all right.'

Sally said nothing. Matt walked across the room and glanced idly through the inspection panel and then stiffened.

'When did that happen?'

'About ten minutes ago. We had problems; one leg was in the wrong position and I had to straighten it.'

'*You* straightened it?' Matt stared at his wife in amazement.

'I used to help with the calving cows when we were snowed up at home,' Sally said. She grinned suddenly. 'Don't look so shattered, Matt. It's not so difficult when you know what to do, and the leg was only a little bit out of place.'

'Are they both all right?' Matt asked. He didn't want to go in and see the aftermath of birth. Donald would have foaled the mare if he hadn't hurt his arm. Matt only came in afterwards, when everything was tidy again.

'They won't be if I don't get on.' Sally's voice was brisk. Poor Matt. It had been a rotten night. But there were worse troubles at sea. The foal was strong. She was already struggling to her legs, her head seeking for the udder. Nothing wrong there.

Sally went back into the foaling room, taking the gruel with her. The mare struggled to her own feet, and stood, feeding eagerly. She nudged the foal against her expertly. She had done it all before. The small mouth found the udder and began to suck. The furry tail waved ecstatically.

The man who had come in to make coffee returned to the office.

'Mr Keene sent me to clear up for you,' he said. 'The mare knows me. I've been helping look after her for the past few weeks. Can I go in?'

Sally went in with him. Fan was busy, too busy to bother with mere humans. She continued to lick her foal while Sally bathed her hind-quarters and towelled her dry, and then towelled the foal to clean her off too.

The man worked swiftly, competently and silently, clearing up the soiled straw, replacing it with dry bedding, bringing another small feed, with a little brandy added, and then bringing the warm rug that would keep Fan from feeling any chill as an aftermath of birth. Sally found packs ready in a drawer, and heated them and put them on the mare. She was swollen and sore from straining and these would ease her.

Neil Lytton was used to the procedure. He brought fresh packs, and helped with them, and then suggested that he stayed with the mare while Sally bedded down for an hour or so on the camp bed in the office. She was glad to comply. Exhaustion had claimed her, swiftly and unexpectedly, so that she felt as if she were sleep walking. Neil brought her coffee, but she was already asleep. He moved his hand to put the blanket across her, but Sheikh bared his teeth and growled from his new position beside his mistress's bed. Neil turned up the fire instead, putting on another electric bar.

Later, Matt came in and put the blanket over his wife.

'I'll stay with the mare,' he said, and Neil went off to help clear up the chaos caused by the night, and soothe frightened horses, and make yet more coffee using the kettle in the office. Sally woke to find a cup steaming beside her bed. She felt stiff and aching all over, and she had been so tired she had not even removed the overalls. She eased herself out of them, drank the coffee, and went to look at the mare and the foal.

'Both fine,' Matt said. He was looking at her as if he had never seen her before. 'I didn't think you had it in you.'

'I've never had the chance,' Sally said. 'Joe never lets anyone else near his mares. But I think I'll have to put my foot down and make him let me help. There might be another night like this; there might be a time when he's ill. And he isn't getting any younger.'

'I'd not have thought it a job for a woman. Didn't the mare panic?'

'Not really. She got a bit wild, but we had wilder animals on our farm. The big Shires were a handful, especially the stallion. I was the only one that could groom him after Gramp died, without blindfolding him first. Animals trust me. I suppose because I grew up with them.'

She was suddenly closer to Matt than she had been for months. He yawned, and bit into a ham sandwich, and looked out into the yard.

'There's a fair old mess out there,' he said. 'But we all need more sleep. As soon as we've done the horses I'll send the lads off for a while. They can leave some of the tidying until later. I wonder how Donald is?'

'Talk of the devil,' Myra said, opening the door. Donald followed her, his arm in plaster.

'Out of action for a while,' Donald said ruefully. Like Matthew, he walked over to the door and glanced into the foaling room at the mare.

'Hey, when did that happen? What is it?'

'A filly – Sally did it all alone,' Matt said, and unexpectedly chuckled. 'It had a bent leg and she straightened it. Learning things about my wife, all the time,' he added.

'It's about time,' Myra said acidly. 'Right now she looks as if she needs a bath and a long long sleep. Come on, Sally love, you've done your whack for the night and so have I. It's Saturday. Some of the men in the village have promised to come and help clear up our mess. Some of them are up at one of the farms, where they had a worse night than us with a barn carried away and a cow killed, and a gate blown down and the whole herd running in blind panic.'

'I hope they don't end up here,' Matt said, yawning. 'I don't need cows to add to the fun. The yearlings are still edgy and they're enough of a handful.'

That evening, Sally went out to look at the mare. Fantasia greeted her with a rub of the head against the woman's shoulder, and watched proudly as the foal came on spindly legs, to investigate the hand that was held out to it. There was honey on Sally's fingers, and the foal licked, identifying the human with pleasure.

Matt was busy with the books in the office.

'Joe's bought that horse,' he said. 'We'll put him on the other side of the house, well away from the mares. A stallion could be a bit of a problem there, but this fellow is gelded. Joe says it's a terrific horse.'

'What's his name?' Sally asked.

'Khazan. It's a name to conjure with. I can't wait to get him home.'

'There's many a slip,' Sally said and laughed, not knowing how true her casual words were to be.

Chapter Three

A passage to England proved difficult to arrange. Very few small boat masters liked taking animals, especially horses, which sometimes panicked, terrified by the sea. The larger boats were all fully booked. Also there was an extensive illicit trade from Ireland to the continent, where horses were still sold for horsemeat, in spite of rules and regulations. The old smuggling instinct never died, and many men felt rules were made to be broken. There was good money from the overseas trade, and money was precious. Horse sales had slumped.

Joe, discovering this, was angry. So angry that he might have beaten up the man who told him, bragging noisily in the pub one night, but Joe had learned at least to keep his temper, even if he did not always watch his tongue. He needed to be fit, and did not want to end in an Irish jail for brawling. He went out, and cooled off on a long walk, but even so he could not drive away the image of beautiful horses sent cynically abroad to be killed and eaten. He tossed in his bed that night, wishing he could alter the world and make men kinder.

He was up early next morning, seeking a man who owned a small charter boat that sometimes carried cattle. He tracked him down at last, sitting on a bollard overlooking the harbour.

'I can take you and the horse day after tomorrow,' Roy Stevens said. 'I came over to load up after tomorrow's horse sales. There'll be a few going back to England. I usually carry cattle, but haven't any this trip. There are six stalls on the boat that'll take horses.'

Joe looked at the vessel. He did not like boats at the best of times, and this one, a rusty tramp that had seen far better days, did little to inspire confidence.

He hesitated.

'It's seaworthy, if that's what you're worrying about,' Roy said. 'A bit of trouble with the engines now and then, but I've just overhauled them. She's OK for at least four trips before they need doing again. I can do the mail boat trip in nearly the same time as the mail boats, given an hour or so.'

'I'll come back,' Joe said, wanting time to think, and time to make enquiries. There was always someone round the docks who knew a boat's history and whether the skipper was to be trusted, or whether he navigated with a bottle of whisky in one hand and his mind on anything but the sea.

'Roy Stevens? He's OK. Won't overcharge, and his boat will get you there. Sure, it isn't pretty. What tramp ever is? He runs it on a shoe string, but he's a good engineer and he overhauls his own boat. No nonsense and won't cheat you either. And he knows animals. Nothing to worry about there.'

Joe thought about flying. It would be quicker, but he trusted planes even less than he trusted the sea. Give him a good firm meadow and a horse beneath him, and he was the most daring man on earth, but at sea or in the air, he was a nervous wreck until they touched land again. He was not an imaginative man except when it came to dying; and death by drowning or death by plane crash seemed to him one of the more undesirable ways to go. He had only flown once, with his eyes shut tight and his fists clenched, feeling sick all the way. When they touched down at Dublin airport he had cancelled his return flight and come home by boat. Even that he hated. Matthew tried to laugh him out of it, but it was no good. Joe had few weaknesses, but his fear of the sea and the air was almost a phobia. He despised himself, but that did little good. His only consolation was that there were many others like him. If it wasn't that he knew Matthew would pay over the odds for any horse, rather than bargain and get it at a reasonable price, Joe would never have left the country.

He came back to Roy that evening, and fixed their passage. He and the horse would be aboard early. It would give Khazan time to settle down before the engines started, and the boat began to toss on the waves. Joe looked out over the sea. It was greeny-grey, surging slowly, a powerful reminder of fear. There were tangled clusters of dark clouds in the sky.

'What about the weather?' Joe asked.

'Piece of cake,' Roy said, scornful of a landsman's idea of bad weather. It would need to blow a hurricane before he regarded it as rough. 'No need to worry. We won't have any bother. We'll travel easily and be across before you know we've started.'

Joe, with memories of rough passages and sea-sickness behind him, very much doubted that. He had some tablets to take, but they made him dopey. He wasn't sure which would be worse; to comfort an anxious horse when he was ill, or to sit half doped while it panicked. It might not panic. It might prove rarely steady. But he had to be prepared for the worst; and the worst, when a terrified horse reared and bucked and kicked in a confined space, was appalling. Dan had promised to tranquillise the animal. But tranquillisers didn't always work.

Joe was a dire pessimist when it came to travelling, with or without a horse.

He found the horse accommodation for the night in a brewery stable, where they still delivered locally with a dray and four handsome Shires. He stopped to help groom the animals, missing his own routine. It was a long time since he'd handled heavy horses. These were magnificent, reminding him of his younger days on his father's farm, and the shows every year when he drove four in harness. He still had the rosettes he had won; and an enlarged picture of the last four beauties. One of them had been called Beauty, like Matt's first horse. She'd been a sweet mare, and had lovely foals.

Then the old man died and the death duties were so exorbitant that all the horses were sold. Joe sold the farm. He didn't want to know, if there weren't to be horses. He had gone to Matthew's father, and was almost a partner now. He shared the responsibility and took many of the decisions. The place couldn't be run without him. He knew that. Matthew hadn't the experience yet. Experience took a long time to come; a lifetime. Longer; you never knew more than a fraction of what there was to know.

Dan brought the horse over the evening before they were due to sail. Joe saw the horsebox draw up in the yard and went to open up, and lead the horse out. Khazan walked down the ramp, unafraid. He followed Joe into the stable, and began to tug at the haynet that was ready for him. There was fresh straw on the ground.

'No vices?' Joe asked, thinking of kicking and bucking, or worse.

'No vices. Some funny little ways,' Dan said. 'He's been more of a pet . . .' He broke off and went out without a backward look, leaving half his heart behind him and a great many hopes. He started the engine of the Land-Rover and drove out of the yard without another word to Joe.

Joe watched him go, pity in his eyes. It was the rare man who could live with an animal for six years and not be fond of it, or sorrow when it went. He knew only too well. He glanced at the placid Shires, brooding peacefully in their stalls. Even now, he remembered the wrench it had been to part with his father's animals. Life wasn't fair, ever, and for some it was worse than others. Maybe you made your own hell, in which case Joe hoped he'd done his time.

He watched the horse. It was magnificent, and a bargain. He ought to have paid more . . . For a moment his loyalty faltered, but business was business, and Dan had accepted their price. Been pleased with it.

There was a milking stool in the passage outside the stall, left over from some long-ago day when there had been cows around. Joe sat on it, and the horse, having finished the food in the manger, came to look at this new person who was looking after him, and leaned his head over the half door.

Joe caught his breath.

He thought of the picture of Golden Miller in his room at home. He knew every inch of the wise head; he could almost have drawn the angles of the bones, the set of the eyes under heavy arches, the set of the ears. This horse was a throwback to a relative long-since dead; almost a perfect replica, at least as to his head, of a great hero. Excitement began to build. What's bred in the bone . . .

The Miller had been an all-time great. He'd been supreme until age daunted him and the younger horses gave him best. He'd made a record at Aintree; he'd won the National by five lengths, in a very fast time indeed, having a reserve speed that left every other horse standing.

There were other great horses in Khazan's pedigree too. If this boy was as good as the Miller . . . Joe sat dreaming, of a record crowd and a record horse and a record time; of the roars of excitement as they jumped the last fences and Matt went ahead on Khazan. If only he were as good as the Miller. Or would he need to be better, much better for today's standards? If he were as good today against the competition as the Miller had been . . .

Joe padlocked the stable door and went out to drink to success.

It would be theirs. He had a hunch; he had a pre-knowledge, a feeling of total elation. They'd nurse the horse for stardom. He would be a great horse, one of the best they'd ever bought, or trained. One day.

Joe had three whiskies, and went to bed to dream of fortune.

He woke to a cold grey day and a thin rain falling and worse, a spiteful needling wind. He had a taste in his mouth and the aftermath of depression. OK, so it was a good horse, but he'd been daft the night before. Dreaming dreams like a schoolgirl mooning over a pop idol. All the same, when he saw the horse again, he knew he was right in one thing. If reincarnation were possible, here it was. He was a proud man as he led his new acquisition for the Keene stables down to the docks.

'We'll be away by midday,' Roy Stevens said. 'Nice horse.'

'Nice horse,' Joe agreed, not wishing to say more. Khazan was uneasy, not liking the boat, which was moving uneasily, rolling on a slow swell. Waves broke white outside the harbour. The sea looked very large and very grim, and very rough to Joe.

'Not bad weather at all,' Roy said, checking his engines. He broke off to introduce his daughter, a slim woman who might have been any age from twenty-five to forty.

'May's my mate on board,' Roy said. 'Don't trust anyone else. She's a splendid sailor. And so are both her sons. Ours is a family boat. Don't need anyone else.'

Dave and Paul proved to be eighteen and nineteen, which made May older than she looked. Joe recognised her efficiency as she worked about the deck. She came down to look at the horse.

'He's the only one. Dad boobed,' she said. 'The other men haven't bought, as the horses were withdrawn. None of them reached their reserve price. One beautiful little foal went for fifteen pounds. It was a crying shame.'

'You like horses?' Joe asked.

May nodded. She was dark-haired, and tanned. Her brown eyes assessed Khazan.

'I bet on them,' she said. 'Not much, but enough. My husband was Dad's partner, and we lived well then, when John was alive. But times are bad. Small firms chartered us and a lot of them have vanished. Gone broke. Everything costs so much; spares; repairs; fuel. I can't live on John's insurances, so I've come into business with Dad. I used to help him, as a kid. And I've often sailed with them.'

'What happened to your husband?' Joe asked.

'He was swept overboard in a storm,' May said bleakly. 'I hate the sea, but it's in my blood; a sort of love-hate relationship. It always sounds a lot of nonsense, but it isn't really.' She sighed. 'Time I got back to work.'

Joe added more straw to the stall, and made sure the horse was securely fastened. He would need to watch all the time. A fall; a broken leg . . . and that was the end of a very expensive investment.

He left the horse briefly in order to eat, wondering if that were wise. The sky was a uniform dark grey, the rain falling remorselessly, and to his unskilled eyes, the sea looked wild.

'It's not as bad as it looks,' May said.

Joe didn't believe her. He believed her even less as they eased slowly out of the harbour, the *Daisy May* bucking and tossing like a horse just caught for breaking. Khazan was uneasy, the whites of his eyes showing, as he moved restlessly in his stall. Joe stood beside him, praying that his inside would behave, just this once. He was gratified to find that it did, at least for longer than usual. He was so occupied with soothing the horse that he had little time for anything else.

Khazan did not like the noise of the ship. He did not like the smell of the ship. He did not like the horrible up and down movement of the creaking boards under his hooves. He was tense and unhappy, but he trusted the man who stood beside him, soothing him, talking to him, stroking him, reassuring him. So long as the man did not go away, the horse would be still. Joe knew that if he left the horse there might be trouble. No horse was so stolid that it took at once to a totally new situation.

May, knowing horses, brought down coffee and sandwiches.

'Barometer's dropping,' she said. 'Might be in for a bit of a blow.'

Joe's guts cramped. A sour taste flooded his mouth, and a sick feeling rose in his throat. The horse could stand this; but a real blow . . . did May mean a real blow, or was it just a sailor's term for something not too bad? He didn't know, but he did know that the falling barometer was an ominous sign. Perhaps the sky would clear. Perhaps he wouldn't be sea-sick, not this time. Perhaps the horse would be so steady, even in a storm, that they would have no trouble. Perhaps chickens would lay diamonds and pigs grow sable coats.

'All right, boy, not to worry,' he said, his voice soft and gentle, an automatic response to a startled movement from the horse. 'Not to worry. We'll soon be there.'

He glanced at his watch.

Dear heaven, they had only been at sea for half an hour. Time felt endless. Already he was sure that the pitch and toss was worse, that the boat was being flung like a toy in a child's bath by the waves, was climbing up them slowly, uncertainly, with the wind against her, turning her off course, was rolling down into a trough, with a seesaw movement that seemed unreasonable for any small boat. Why hadn't he flown with the horse? Why on earth hadn't they gone to Newmarket and bought a horse there? He'd have been home by now and safe.

And it was cold. Bitterly cold. Joe shivered, drawing his coat round him more tightly, wishing he had more clothes with him. He sat bleakly, hissing softly to the horse, trying to drown the noise of wind and water with his own thoughts. Somehow they were all unpleasant thoughts; remembering the weeks that followed after Sally's baby died. Matt hadn't thought about his wife at all; only his own grief, almost hating her because she had lost his son through a fault in her blood. No one had dared cross him in those weeks.

Joe had watched Sally wander listlessly about the place, her face white, her eyes enormous in shadowy sockets, longing for a word from Matt. He had never given it to her. More than once Joe had thought of giving his employer a piece of his mind, but it wouldn't have done anything but antagonise Matt further. He was a very difficult man. His father had been difficult too. Joe sometimes wondered if that was why Matt's mother had died young. Women were background to the Keene men. Not partners.

It wouldn't work for ever. Not with Sally. She had recovered from the death of her baby, but she was bitter and frustrated and hurt, and one day she might up and leave. Matthew wasn't aware of that, Joe thought. And maybe Sally wasn't either, but she had no life of her own. She didn't even have the reassurance of being needed to keep house. She was a hostess, and that was all, to be shown off like an Arab mare. Sometimes Joe hated his employer, and now, with the wind screaming above him and the boat lifting and sinking in nightmare movements, he loathed him, and he loathed horses, and he loathed the sea most of all.

Up and down.

Up and down.

On and on, and Joe was a prisoner, tied to the horse, unable to leave the horse, enduring a nightmare of cold and wet, as water now was hurling itself over the deck and rushing down into the hold. There might not be anyone else aboard. Once he climbed the companion ladder, and looked out, horrified by the rush of wild water that crashed about him. The wind tore at his face, taking away his breath.

May, hanging on to the stanchions, wearing oilskins and a lifejacket, came to him, handing him a lifejacket to put on. He stared at her in horror. She said something, but the words were torn from her, floating away on the wind.

There was no longer time to feel sick. Only time to feel fear. What in heaven's name would happen to the horse if they abandoned ship? He couldn't do it. He couldn't leave the horse behind.

Joe went back to sit on the floor, hanging on to a handhold on the gate of the stall. The horse was slithering about, but there was nothing Joe could do. He saw a wild eye, and knew there was a whinny that went with it, and knew that if he went into the stall he would be kicked to death. There was only terror for both of them.

He was flung across the floor, hitting his head. Blood from a cut over his eye masked his vision. There had been a rending clang. He couldn't believe it, but he knew that his ears had heard right as water began to pour into the boat. He could not leave the horse there. He would open the stall and leave him free. Perhaps he would survive, and the boat would survive, even if they abandoned it.

All Joe's nightmares were coming true.

Paul came down the ladder, clinging tightly, rolling with the boat. He stared at the rushing water, and held out a hand to Joe. Joe took it, and made his way on deck. The horse had entered the hold through two large doors that opened, and then were shut. Water was pouring in through these.

'The horse,' Joe yelled.

'No way,' Roy shouted. The lifeboat was launched, and there was no choice. They were listing badly. It was almost

37

impossible to get aboard the tiny craft, but somehow they managed it, and Roy cut the rope that held it.

The *Daisy May* was above them, leaning at a crazy angle. On board was one of the biggest investments that Joe had ever made for Matthew. On board was a beautiful horse that was alive, and afraid, and was being left to die. If only he had a gun he would have shot it and saved it those last terrifying hours of agony. The horse was insured. But what was money? It never replaced flesh and blood, or compensated for suffering.

Joe stared across the sea, oblivious of his own discomfort.

The lifeboat was even worse than the *Daisy May* had been; but his thoughts were all with Khazan, alone in his stall, with no one to soothe him, or feed him, or clean him or comfort him.

Roy passed a flask to Joe, motioning him to drink.

Joe tried, but he couldn't swallow the scalding hot, brandy-laced coffee that had been the last thing May had managed to make. They had lost their boat. It was insured. They would get another, a better boat, maybe, and could go on.

The sea flung them carelessly across the waves. In the far distance another ship changed course and came towards them. Roy set off a flare. It lit the sea and the sky with a weird light, smoking heavily, a plume to point their position. They would be rescued soon. They had foundered in a busy shipping lane.

The horse was insured.

But nothing could make up for his loss.

Nothing could make up for having to leave him alone, in disastrous circumstances, reft from a safe home where he had lived as a pet.

Joe stood, shivering, at the rail when he was hauled aboard the Dutch steamer, refusing to go below and get warm as long as he could see the *Daisy May* wallowing wearily in seas that were surely mountainous.

He felt like Judas.

Chapter Four

Khazan was a curious horse, interested in the world around him. He enjoyed being taken to strange places, and was quite unafraid of the horse box. Dan had sometimes used him to steady a younger animal, putting Zan in the box first. Zan's patient eyes watched the youngster, and the aura of calm emanating from him helped to quieten nerves.

The horse had also been used to steady a windy pony. Zan was quite unafraid of traffic. Dan rode him when he was breaking a new horse for the road, and the older horse turned himself sideways if the young one panicked, interposing his body between the frightening monster that was roaring up to them, shielding the youngster. No one taught him to do so. He took it on himself to teach that cars stayed on the road and were harmless. He had never been hurt by a vehicle and trusted them all, blindly.

He had followed Joe without fear, recognising that this man knew horses. It was not the first time he had gone away from Dan. Nor the first time he had left the stables and stayed in a strange place overnight. He watched the Shire horses in the brewery stables with interest and nosed the mare in the next stall, liking the scent of her.

He had not liked entering the boat. The docks were noisier than anything he had encountered before. There were cranes lifting huge packs above him, and he was afraid that something might drop on him. He did not like the wet slippery weedy jetty, or the waves that broke over his hooves, but he trusted Joe and followed him quietly, bracing himself against the unexpected uneasy movement of the boat.

The doors in the hold had clanged shut behind him, leaving him in the dark. Someone switched on a light, and the horse had stared about him, nostrils working overtime at the sea scent, eyes rolling as the boat tossed. The engine sound was strange and he did not like that either, but Joe was beside him, telling him that he was safe, that it did not matter, that there was nothing to fear. The soft voice soothed him; the gentle hand was comfort; so long as the man was there, nothing would go wrong.

The rending sound panicked the horse. Joe had been flung across the boat and vanished, and then, mysteriously, Joe was gone and Zan was alone, and the gate of his stall open, swinging wildly to and fro. Water was pouring in; water that spilled round his feet, water that splashed and soaked him.

He was surrounded by noise; the wild shriek of the wind; the surge and roar and bellow of the rolling waves, the grinding, creaking noise of the huge doors in front of him. They had been struck by the wreckage of another ship, which had been abandoned an hour before, as she too was flooding. Waterlogged, she had rocked dangerously, a menace to all other boats. The hold doors had been hit with a sideways bang that had unseated the bolts that held them. The great ram across the doors had snapped, as if made of matchwood.

The lights went out.

The engine died.

The *Daisy May* was wallowing clumsily, rolling on the waves. Zan panicked. His flailing hooves struck the doors, which were already creaking open with the weight of the water inside the boat.

The doors flung wide.

The boat rolled.

Khazan lost his footing and was in the water, was outside the boat, was trapped beneath it, was sinking down, struggling for breath, his lungs crying out for air. Water filled his eyes and ears and nostrils. It was bitterly cold, and he was drowning, sucked into a swirl that he could not fight.

The *Daisy May* rolled away from him.

The suck of water had gone. He rose to the surface, long legs flailing wildly, his tortured lungs taking in great gulps of air.

The need to live, the need to fight the terror that engulfed him, was all that he had left. He began to swim, his powerful legs striking out automatically, although he had never been in water before.

It was blind instinct, fighting for survival. Fighting for the safe land beneath his hooves. Fighting against the waves that swamped him, against the wind that tossed the water, against the objects floating around him that hit him and bruised his body.

He had no sense of time.

He swam.

The wind died, all the waves were quieter, and the night was succeeded by the gleam of grey at dawn; Khazan could see the waves that tossed him, could see the deep troughs between them, could see the sky brighten and lighten and the sun shine through.

He was alone in a waste of water, bruised, weary, and very hungry. If he went on there would be men and there would be food. There always had been men and there always had been food, every day of his life. It could not end now. Somewhere men were waiting. He only had to find them. They were not thinking thoughts in his head; only feelings; instincts that told him to go on, not to give up, to fight against this horrible creature that was trying to kill him. He would always fight; if he were wild he would fight other stallions; if he were put with rivals he would fight to the death, because it was in him never to give up, always to go on, always to face a challenge.

He had faced the jumps, ever higher and higher.

He had run a race when his heart was pounding in him and breath bursting in him, and the ground rock-hard and the other horses pressing him. But he had to win, had to go all out, whatever he did, always. He had all the arrogance of all the winners that made up his heredity; of the great Miller himself, who had always given his best. He had to go on, even when lightning lanced the sky and wild thunder rolled across the sullen waves, and the crash in his ears seemed endless and no hope was left.

He swam.

He was a small speck in a vast wasteland. He was flotsam, floating on the water. Only one man saw him, and did not realise that he was looking at a horse. He had been on watch for all of the night, and he saw a small speck disappear between the waves, and thought it was a block of wood. Khazan was unaware of the boat that had almost run him down.

He swam.

His legs ached with effort. His breath rasped in his throat. His lungs were sore. He had swallowed an ocean of water. He did not know where he was going, or why he was there, or why men had deserted him. He did not know why he was swimming. He did not know he could stop, give up and sink beneath the waves. Instinct had taken over. Instinct that made him go on, and on, and on. That forced his weary body into even more effort, breasting each wave more slowly now, almost drifting down into the trough, and then up again.

He did not know that he was being helped by a current that set to the shore when the tide had turned.

He did not know what would happen to him.

He was an automaton, going on relentlessly, even though his efforts were feebler. He was nearing exhaustion and the time would come when even he could not conquer the wind and the sea and the cold.

The time had not come yet.

The sun had risen in the sky. He was aware of hunger; he longed for food and for clean fresh water; for hay, and for a soothing hand to say, 'It's all right, old boy. Not to worry. It'll soon be over.'

Nobody came.

He was alone for ever in a millrace, where the waves broke white over his sodden head, and the water took him like a toy and pushed him about and he could master nothing.

He swam.

The tide was flooding, the current was faster, helping him, but Khazan was not aware of that. He was aware of nothing but the need to go on, to breast the waves, to keep his legs moving, striking out ever more feebly, aching with exhaustion, beyond hunger. Almost beyond caring.

He had been in the water for over ten hours. Far behind him, the *Daisy May* lolled, waterlogged, rocking on a sea now much calmer. Joe had reported that they were safe, over the radio, and asked for the horse to be rescued. The rescue ship arrived. The hold doors had closed again, but the hold was flooded deep. No horse floated on the water. Either he was trapped there, dead, or had somehow been flung out into the heaving seas. Either way, there was no hope for him.

Joe was bitterly disappointed. The horse was insured, but that wasn't the point. He had failed Matt and although the loss wasn't his fault, as the storm had been unpredicted and quite exceptional, he never forgave himself.

No one looked for the horse.

Khazan was no longer swimming. He was floating, drifting with the tide, sinking under the water and struggling wearily to the surface again, refusing to accept water that choked him and hurt his lungs; that stung his eyes, that flooded into his ears. He tried to shake his head. He could not see clearly, because he needed to keep his eyes closed against the stinging salt.

He could not go on.

His legs would not work any more. He was a feeble piece of flotsam, drifting with the seaweed.

The wind from the land strengthened. It blew towards the horse.

The smells around him changed.

There was salt and weed and the sharp sea tang, but there was grass, and cattle and woodsmoke. There was a smell like the smell of the stables in Ireland; there were people, somewhere near him. There was hope.

The will to survive strengthened him and he struck out again, with bolder movements of his legs, towards the shore. The tide was full, and soon would turn. The sea had quietened. There were rocks all around him, with fierce fangs that threatened him, but he was unaware of danger, even though one spike raked his leg, cutting it. He was not conscious of the blood that flowed into the water, and did not even notice the sting of the sea in the wound.

There was land.

There was grass, and he would be able to feed.

There were gulls winging about him, calling, diving to look at this unlikely swimmer, wondering if it was food. They annoyed him, and he tried to change direction, away from the insistence of swooping wings and beaks he was

43

afraid might stab at his eyes. He had never seen sea birds before.

He was rocking with the water. He was heading towards a narrow cove, high cliffs shielding it on either side from the weather, trapping the sun, so that it was warm and a favourite place for some of the village children, and for some of those older too, to bask and swim, and lie against the rocks, lazing. Few of them bothered, but there were a small number who knew the cove. Summer visitors never found it. Shallow steps led down the steep cliff, to the rocks that were tumbled around at the head of the beach.

Khazan touched bottom. He could walk, instead of swimming. He moved slowly, almost done for. He stumbled wearily among rocks that trapped him, and tried to swim again, but the water was too shallow now. He came through the waves, soaked, bedraggled, defeated, his head hanging low, too heavy to lift. Once he fell, and lay for a while with the water creaming over his body, while he breathed deeply. A wave came and covered his head, and he struggled up again and walked on, now picking his way delicately among the rocks. There was some sand; that was kind to his hooves.

He was out of the water and on the beach and the sun was setting behind the cliffs. The sky rioted with colour. Dark clouds were slashed with crimson and the light reflected in the water, dying it red.

The light changed the colour of Zan's soaked coat. He was a glowing horse for one moment as he stood, sniffing.

He moved uncertainly, stumbling, pausing between each step. He reached the edge of the cove, where sparse grass grew on the banks of a stream that tumbled down the cliffs. He bent his head to the water.

It was sweet, clean, and fresh.

It was elixir, as he drank, washing away the salt in his mouth and throat. He stood in it, feeling it clear and cold round his hooves.

He cropped at the grass but he had no energy to feed.

He had no energy left at all.

He stretched himself on the sand beneath the cliffs, and lay like a dead horse, sleeping soundly, totally exhausted. The breath that moved his chest was uneven, and fluttered. He did not know that if no one came he would die there, needing food and warmth. The blood still oozed from the cut on his leg.

The birds watched him, waiting, knowing what he did not know.

A small wind needled his mane, but he did not even open his eyes. He had fought to the last, and time was running out for him, fast.

The wild birds knew. The hungry gulls perched on the cliffs all night.

Chapter Five

Morning dawned, bitter chill in spite of the season, and grey. The horse did not move. He lay sleeping, halfway between living and dying, knowing nothing. Beyond, the gulls waited, patient. They could wait for hours if need be. Their time would come.

High on the cliffs, above Khazan, Samuel Trelawny was picking flowers for the market. He held the blossoms delicately in powerful hands. At the end of each row he handed them to Debbie, his daughter, who counted them into tens and bunched them. Her heart was not in her work. She had recently been very ill, and the rheumatic fever that almost killed her had left her weak and breathless.

Her father watched her from under dense eyebrows that bristled above his dark eyes. He was a solemn man, never laughing, dedicated to his religion, which was his only consolation since his young wife had died when their child was born.

It had been his fault that the child was born; sinning against God. Elizabeth had been a delicate girl, but so beautiful. Even now, fourteen years later, he could not remember her without a catch in his throat. It was easy to remember her. Deborah was too like her mother for her father's comfort. A turn of the head, a smile, a wayward flirt of the wind in the long fair hair that was always covered by the scarf that all women of his religion had to wear out of doors, and his wife was reincarnated daily.

Samuel knew that a man made his own hell. He tried to save Debbie from the same hell, bringing her up in God's name, praying with her night and morning, keeping her, as much as was possible, from worldly sin.

That was easy as there was little money to spare for extra labour and he needed his daughter's help with the flowers. She was good at making wreaths and garlands and bouquets and although Samuel thought all but the wreaths were frivolous, flowers were his business, and he needed money to buy food and extra comforts for the child now. She was white as their nanny goat and had so little energy that he was terrified she would fade on him, as her mother had. He insisted on feeding her with beef broth and marrow-bone broth and chicken broth, until Debbie thought she would gurgle with liquid and longed for more solid food.

She placed the bunches of flowers in the baskets, counting them carefully, ready for her father to take them in his van to the station and put them on the train for London. He worked endlessly and his flowers were bigger and stronger than other growers' flowers. All his spare time went into his work. There was little leisure.

Only enough for prayer.

Samuel looked across at the child. It was hard for a man to be left with a girl child and he was a stern father, wanting her to grow up sensible and hard-working, not like the flighty girls he saw in the towns when he went to stock the pantry, or the shameless hussies that flaunted their bodies in next to nothing on the beaches. He was appalled by them, and drove home swiftly, eyes on the road, ignoring the hitch-hikers. Asking for trouble, the wicked little trollops. He was still a man, for all his religion which was bitter and intense and entirely of his own making, and although he would never take another wife, or have dealings with another woman, he had all a man's feelings, try as he would to stifle them, and pray as he would for peace at night.

Debbie was a quiet child, thrown entirely on her own for company. Her father only spoke of work, or of religion and of duty. She knew, from her school friends, that she led a strange life; and she had no pretty clothes. Her skirts and blouses and jerseys did for school as well as for home. Her skirts were always too long; and only on the games field did she dare to appear without a covering on her hair, and even then she felt guilty.

She was not allowed to visit other children. Their homes might contaminate her and make her discontented. She listened in astonishment to the tales which other children saw nightly on television. She could not imagine it, and once, when her father left her to wait for him outside a seed merchant's, she had wandered down the street and discovered a shop that sold radios and television sets and stared at the moving pictures in amazement, until Samuel, coming out and finding her gone, had looked for her and scolded her angrily.

Her only companions were the animals at the cottage. Bibi, the goat, Snowy, the little owl that she had rescued when he fell from the nest; Mop, her dog, another stray that had been born in the ditch. Her father had drowned the bitch and four of the pups, but Debbie had cried so much he had relented and let her keep the strongest. It was a fluffy nondescript pup, all fur, well deserving its name. And there was also Nini, the little cat that had produced kittens in the shed, and had been allowed to stay, because Debbie was so ill and nothing tempted her. The kittens made her laugh. She had cuddled them, and played with them, and come back from the gateway that led to something Samuel could only imagine. That night he had thanked God for his mercy and the cat had found a home.

Even so, the child had no strength in her, and Samuel, watching her, was afraid she might yet slip away from him.

He straightened his back wearily. The pain at the base of his spine was constant now, reminding him that he was not immortal and if anything happened to him, what would happen to his girl? Maybe one of the Brethren would take her in and teach her the way she should go. He caught his breath as the pain came again. Disc trouble the doctor had said, when he went for advice, against his religion, but there was the child to think of. Not that the advice helped, with all the flowers to pick and no money to pay a hired hand,

and the early crop killed by frost, which had savaged this corner of Cornwall for the first time in Samuel's memory.

'Time to rest,' Samuel said, watching the child's weary movements and wishing he knew how to tell her how much she meant to him. Sometimes she looked at him as if she hated him; as if he were a stranger, determined to thwart her all the time. But she was too pretty for her own good, and she must learn to know how beauty could trap a man; she must be hidden in thick ungainly clothes, hair dragged back into a tight pigtail, her natural exuberance curbed. There at least he was succeeding. She was much quieter now. Once he had worried because she was so excitable. She had cried over the dead pups, as if the end of the world were about to come.

Mop was frisking in the sunshine on the cliff top. Debbie walked over to the dog, and called him, but he was staring down into the cove. There were birds on the rocks and beyond them was something he could smell; something alive; some animal. Mop had never seen a horse. He was never taken away from the little flower farm. He guarded it when Debbie and her father were both away.

Debbie knelt beside the dog and held him against her, but he broke away, needing to find out, having intense curiosity. His small round body bumped down the steps, and Debbie followed him, while her father sat on the big rock that cropped out in the middle of his land, and drank his coffee, and eased himself to allay the pain in his back.

Mop reached the sand at the bottom of the steps and trotted across it, and sniffed the giant animal that lay there. He backed off, and barked.

Khazan opened an eye, and flicked an ear.

Debbie saw the movement.

For the first time for days her interest was roused. She ran down the last few steps, and arrived, panting, beside the horse. She stared down at him. He was damp from sea water, his mane and tail crusted with salt, his eyes almost closed, his hide raw from the stinging wind and waves, his lips rough with scaly skin that would soon form into sores.

He stared up at her, unable to move, not caring about danger, aching in every muscle of his body.

The long gash on his flank was red and oozing blood.

Debbie called.

Wearily, Samuel raised himself to his feet and hurried over to the cliff edge, afraid she might have fallen. She was kneeling on the ground below him, beside a horse.

A horse?

Samuel stared at it, bewildered. It must have fallen over the cliff, having strayed from some farm. There were no horses near. He hurried down the steps, cursing the pain in his back.

'Father. Look!' Debbie said.

'The poor beast's come from the sea.' Samuel bent over the animal, and Khazan looked at the man, a trusting look, that said now all would be well; he was among men again. The knowledge that men could be cruel had not come to Khazan. No one had been unkind to him in all of his life. He moved his head, and laid his muzzle gently against the man's hand, and Samuel, staring down at the animal, felt a sudden bond. He had owned a horse of his own once, long ago. Before his father died and his mother married again and his stepfather, a stern man, a minister of a very strict Christian sect, had used both a horse whip and a scathing tongue to teach his stepson how to behave in a world that he thought was increasingly vicious and rotten.

'Will he die?' Debbie asked.

'Fetch a rope,' Samuel said.

He watched the light come into the child's eyes, and thought how easy it was to please her. A puppy. A kitten. A baby owl. Sometimes when nights were long and dark, he agonised, lest he be wrong and the rest of the world be right, and he were denying the child rights that belonged to her. But she did not hanker after pretty things; after worldly things; she hankered only after natural things. He never grudged her flowers for the house. She loved to touch them, to arrange them, and though he thought them frivolous, in spite of his occupation, he had to admit that the child could conjure beauty out of a few stems, and that she had an eye for colour and for shape and for pattern.

He knelt by the horse, a very confused man, remembering those long-ago days, and his own pony, a black pony with a flowing mane and tail. He had only been six years old when his father died. They had lost everything, as the stables were rented; and the horses had to go to give them an income. There had been a riding accident. Samuel shook his head to clear his thoughts. No use remembering the past. Only try to do your best with the present. And to save the child from heartbreak.

Debbie had returned with a bucket, in which were long stems of green grass that she had sheared from the edge of the ditch. She laid them on the ground, and filled the bucket with fresh water and brought it to the horse. Khazan staggered to his feet, swaying, and bent his head to drink. Debbie put her arms around him, willing him to grow strong, and to live.

But the struggle had been too hard.

The horse fell to the ground, and stared up at them, bewildered by his own weakness. Debbie knelt, her arms around his neck.

'Come on,' she whispered. 'You can. I know you can. I know what it feels like. I've been ill. Legs all jelly and you can't get your breath. Come on, fellow. Please come on. You'll be all right. Just try.'

The horse knew she wanted to help him. He tried again to stand, and this time he ate a few of the grass stems that Debbie held out to him. She had her sandwiches in her pocket. She had made bread the night before for her father, who had insisted she took food. She hadn't wanted it, but she never liked to disappoint Samuel, and obediently made herself a pack, intending to feed it to Mop. Khazan caught the smell of new-baked bread and nosed her pocket.

She opened the pack and held a sandwich out to him. He nuzzled it, and she removed the meat and gave him the crust. New-baked bread brought memory. He had stolen it so often from Dan's kitchen table, when the window was open. He nudged Debbie with his head, wanting more, feeling strength come slowly back to his legs.

'We'll have to get him up the cliff,' Samuel said. 'The tide's turning. He'll be trapped.'

He had made a halter from the rope.

Debbie looked at the cliff, at the steps cut in it; at the sea, coming ever closer, rougher now that the tide had turned, with the wind behind blowing white caps off the waves. The sea would surge into the cove within less than half an hour now; would pound against the cliffs, would batter the horse mercilessly.

'Come on, boy, you've got to come on,' Debbie said urgently, fear the only emotion she now had left. She pulled on the halter.

Khazan could barely move.

He was so stiff and aching from his long swim and so weak from the long immersion in the water. One step followed another, slowly, hesitantly, with Samuel beside the horse, his arms around the animal's neck, then moving behind the horse to try and push him, praying he wouldn't kick.

'It's not that he won't come,' Samuel said. 'He can't. We'll have to leave him, or we'll be drowned too.'

The water was creeping towards them, was breaking high on the rock spit, was threatening them with a brutal death. Not just drowning, but battering against the rocky teeth that jagged everywhere.

'The cruel crawling sea,' Debbie whispered under her breath. 'Please God, let the horse walk; help us get him up the cliff; please God, I don't often ask you for anything; and this is for a life. He's beautiful.'

He looked anything but beautiful. Samuel thought perhaps he was an old nag that someone hadn't wanted and had thrown into the sea, cruelly, not wanting to pay for his destruction. There was nothing about the horse to show his youth or his breeding. There was only the bruised body, the soaked mane and tail, the red-rimmed eyes, the froth-flecked mouth, and the harsh breathing.

Water crashed on the rock, flinging spray over all of them.

Khazan had escaped once from the sea.

The horse turned his head and saw the waves trying to catch him again, and began to move slowly, carefully, one hoof in front of another, as if each movement required immense thought and immense effort. He slipped on wet seaweed, and Debbie cried out. She was fighting tears as her father hated tears, not knowing how to deal with them. She blinked furiously, and bit her lip, determined not to be a baby.

Khazan came to the steps. They wound up the cliff, high above him. He had never seen steps before.

The sea was beneath them, was coming towards them, was reaching out for them, was creaming round his hooves, was soaking Debbie's shoes, and Samuel's trousers. He pushed the horse and Debbie pulled the horse, and tentatively, fearfully, Khazan stepped up.

Nothing happened.

The ground was solid. Only he was at an odd angle, two legs up and two legs down, and the sea again reaching up for him, splashing him, terrifying him. He moved again.

Up and up, endlessly, wearily, with Samuel's back a fiery ache as he pushed against the horse; and Debbie, tears flooding down her cheeks, sure that they would never reach the top, that the horse would die before they got there, that her father would collapse. She knew his back was bad, and she was aware that he gasped at every step, and also that when they got to the top there were still flowers to pack, and the van to drive and the train to catch. And she had orders to fulfil; for a death in the village; for an unknown bride; flowers for the reception and for the church; flowers for bouquets and headpieces for bride and bridesmaids; flowers for buttonholes. It was a good job she had been ill and was not yet well enough to return to school, as otherwise she would have had to sit up doing the work all evening, after her lessons were finished. She was always so tired . . .

One step after another. One hoof after another. Up and on. A struggle for all of them, working together, willing themselves to the top. If the horse survived she would call it Blaze, as it had a white mark between its ears, stretching down the soft muzzle. It looked dreadful, a scarecrow of a horse. How had it got into the water?

Push and pull and heave.

Up and up and on.

Until at last, when the horse was ready to drop again, and Debbie so exhausted that she could not even see properly and Samuel was aware of almost nothing but his back, they stood together on soft green grass, and the sea was far below them, its noise muted to a whisper, the spray gleaming in the sunshine in a mazy lace of spume that flung itself fountainwise, high in the air, and fell again as the waves crashed endlessly against the resisting rocks.

The horse moved ever more slowly, until he was away from the dangerous edge of the cliff, and there Samuel let him drop again, this time easing himself down, instead of falling. Debbie took the weary head in her arms and held it, willing the animal to live, to grow strong, to become hers.

Samuel looked down at them. He did not dare to sit. If he did, he would never get up again. He needed help. He couldn't go on and it was insane to try. He couldn't let this horse die. The past had risen to mock him; and then he wondered if it were mockery, and not comfort, remembering a time long ago when he had been happy. Was happiness wrong?

'Can I keep the horse?' Debbie asked. She knew it was a stupid question and that her father would say no. They had no money to spare for a horse. But they did have a disused stable beside the old barn. They lived in an old farmhouse, although they grew flowers in the fields, and not agricultural crops. The rest of the land had been sold. Times were hard. There would be grass to graze soon; they could buy in enough hay to tide them over. She looked up at her father.

He stood, exasperated, seeing not her but her mother; the same obstinate expression; the same blue eyes; the same fair hair, hidden under the ugly scarf. Several strands had escaped and were blowing across the child's face. It was very hard for Debbie to keep tidy.

Sam swallowed.

'If the horse lives,' he said. It was a safe promise. He had never seen such an exhausted animal. They would do their best for it, and there wasn't much hope that it could survive. 'But don't bank on it.'

'He needs the vet,' Debbie said. Her father had called the doctor to her when she was ill, although it was against his beliefs. The horse couldn't survive without professional help.

'No,' Sam said, and turned away. He had broken the rules once and he wasn't going to again. He still felt guilty. Maybe God had intended Debbie to die, and he had no right to her. He was tired, and he wished he had a wife, and he felt confused. This time, it would be different. It was an animal, not a human life.

Debbie watched her father walk away.

She looked at the horse. He had closed his eyes and was sleeping, the breath slowly lifting his chest. The climb up the cliffs had been too much for him, after his ordeal. She could only guess at that.

He was dying, in spite of their efforts.

Debbie lay beside Khazan, hoping to comfort him, feeling the wetness of him, seeing the tangles in his mane and tail. Her tears added to his soaked coat but he did not feel them. He felt nothing. He lay, balanced between death and life, nearer to death, while the sun shone and the waves beat on the shore and the hungry gulls waited.

Chapter Six

Three boats sank in the storm in which the *Daisy May* was lost. Also, that night, there was an explosion on a large tanker. The resulting oil slick was the source of major news. No one mentioned the *Daisy May*. Joe Garnery was sure the horse had drowned. They claimed on the insurance and Khazan became an expensive might-have-been. No one thought of looking for him. No animal could have swum in those mountainous seas.

Samuel Trelawny asked around, but no one had lost a horse. The animal was a sorry-looking object, worn by his ordeal, his coat dull with salt. Sam suspected some callous farmer had thrown him into the sea to drown, rather than pay for his destruction. Only Khazan knew the truth and he was unable to talk.

He lay exhausted in the straw in the dilapidated stable. Sam looked at the animal, sure it would die anyway. It would be absurd to keep a horse. There was little enough spare money as it was, but Debbie had set her heart on getting the animal well, and she had always been crazy about horses. When she was seven she had had a dream pony, Silver, a gentle little mare with a red saddle and bridle. Sometimes Sam could have almost sworn that the pony really existed. It dominated more than two years of their lives.

Debbie spent every moment she had trying to get the salt out of the horse's coat. They had rubbed him dry and bathed his eyes and nose and ears and he had rewarded Debbie with a push of his head against her shoulder, so thankful to be safe on shore, and be looked after again. He had never had to fend for himself in his life.

The hours in the sea had drained away his strength. He tried to feed, but had little appetite. Debbie fought to interest him in living. He was her talisman; she would work on the farm, and work in the village at the little café in summer to get money to pay for his keep. Keep him she would. He was the materialisation of a dream, and Debbie was as stubborn as her father.

The postman, coming into the yard with a sheaf of bills for Sam, stopped to look into the stable, having heard all about their find. He stroked the soft neck.

'He's not going to make it, Debbie,' he said. 'Don't bank on it, girl. Your dad ought to get the vet.'

Debbie swallowed the lump that appeared just now to be a permanent fixture in her throat. She knew the horse was weaker. One of the cuts on his leg looked as if it were going septic and she did not like the way he breathed. She had argued with her father only that morning over breakfast.

'You know dad,' Debbie said.

Johnnie Masters did know Sam. Johnnie was a married man with two daughters about Debbie's age. They ran free on the cliffs, swam in the cove, romped in bathing costumes on the sands. He had never seen Debbie play. She had always been a solemn child, helping around the place, far too old for her age.

'Maybe I can do something,' Johnnie said. It angered him to see the animal suffering with help only a mile away. Michael Pope, the vet, was on Johnnie's round and there were letters to be delivered. The postman wasn't a man to interfere, but where children and animals were involved,

Johnnie was a sucker. Everyone knew where to go when a stray kitten or a pup needed a home.

Sam was busy in the fields that afternoon when a tall, fair-haired boy wheeled his bicycle into the yard and leaned it against the stable door. He looked around him curiously, at the worn cobbles, at the ancient barn, at the big greenhouses that were so neatly kept; at the stable, a memory of former glory. It hadn't housed a horse for at least twenty years. Sam had boarded up the worst gaps, but it still looked to Bob Pope as if it might fall down.

Debbie recognised Bob. She had often seen him riding in and out of the vet's house, both on his bicycle and on the bay hunter that she wished, so often, was hers.

'Johnnie told me about your find. Can I see him?' Bob asked. 'It's not every day you find a horse coming out of the sea like Venus out of the waves. Perhaps he's a god. Phoenix would be a good name for him.'

Debbie smiled uncertainly, overwhelmed by Bob's easy confidence. It must be wonderful to be like that she thought enviously, praying that he wouldn't turn to her and say something damning like 'cat got your tongue?' as old Mrs Hannitance at the corner shop was apt to do, when she found it difficult to make conversation.

'Johnnie says he's in a bad way.'

Debbie nodded miserably as she opened the stable door. The horse looked at them apathetically. Bob just prevented himself from whistling in dismay. It was almost cruelty to leave the animal like that. They had done their best. The horse was rugged in two thin blankets, obviously taken from a bed; the floor was clean and swept, the straw fresh and the food good; but the horse needed antibiotics; he needed skilled attention, and though Sam had dressed the wounds on the legs, one gash needed a stitch and another showed signs of infection. Also the stable was draughty. It would cause even more problems if there was a sudden temperature drop at night, and that was on the cards too at this time of year.

'Dad won't let me call your father in. He doesn't believe in vets or doctors,' Debbie said. 'And I haven't enough money of my own to pay.' She put her arms round the horse so that Bob shouldn't see her face.

'There's one thing we could do,' Bob said. 'I've some medicines with me that we used on my own horse when he was very ill. There's enough left over for yours. Only one dose is needed. It won't do him any harm at all, I promise, and it might do some good. I brought it with me when Johnnie said how ill the horse was. Your father needn't even know.'

It was deceitful and wrong, and Debbie hesitated, but then she looked at the horse, at his heaving sides and the tiny shiver that occasionally racked him. She nodded again, not trusting her voice.

Bob had decanted the brandy into a medicine bottle, knowing Sam's views on drink. Everyone in the village knew. It was labelled 'one dose only to be given', and the bottle was half full. Debbie held the horse's head as Bob poured the liquid down, praying that it would work. If not, perhaps he could smuggle in a syringe; his father would help him if a sick animal were involved. Never mind payment. Michael Pope was a dedicated man.

The horse swallowed and choked and swallowed and spluttered, but the brandy went down. He swallowed again. And again, and again. Debbie cradled the animal's wise-eyed head in her arms. The coat was dry now. Bob Pope looked at the animal, suspecting the truth. This was no ordinary horse. In spite of his condition, he was a thorough-bred. He looked as if he would be a magnificent animal when he was fit.

'I wonder if someone stole him and ran off?' Bob said and then wished he hadn't, as Debbie looked up at him, her face desperately unhappy.

'Then he'll be advertised for,' she said.

'I'll listen out,' Bob said. 'Carry on. You're doing a great job, but it would be easier if my dad could have a look at him and treat him. He'd get better much more quickly. Can't you persuade your dad?'

'I've argued and argued,' Debbie said, hating her father at that moment, and feeling guilty because of it. Sam had called the doctor when she was ill; but this was different. Why did their religion forbid interference with nature? She hated God too; how could any deity be so cruel?

'I just can't make him see,' she said forlornly.

Bob put the medicine bottle in the pocket of his anorak. The horse was looking brighter already. Brandy could work miracles, but Bob suspected this horse was beyond that. He sat on the low stone wall with Debbie. She ought to be helping her father pick flowers; she had taken too much time off in the last two days, but she knew if she went down to Sam she would rail at him, furious with him because of his obstinacy. If only she had some money of her own; if only she could call the vet on her own responsibility.

Bob said nothing, knowing the turmoil in Debbie's mind. No use him talking to Sam. It would be impertinence. And Sam prided himself in keeping himself to himself and asking help from no one.

There was a rustle from the stable as Sam came into the yard. The horse had decided to stand. His legs were rubbery, and he felt very weak, but Bob had a piece of carrot in his pocket. The horse loved carrots. He took it gently, nibbling it as Debbie held it in her fingers.

'Someone's taught him nice manners,' Sam said, knowing Debbie was angry with him, and wanting to soothe her. 'He'll be all right now, girl. Give him a haynet and go and get some rest. I'll need you later to help pack the flowers.'

'He's a lovely horse,' Debbie said determinedly. She looked up at her father. 'He's got a white mark down the centre of his nose. I'm going to call him Blaze.'

'Looks like he could be a good jumper,' Bob said. 'You might be able to ride him in local gymkhanas. They're fun. I ride in them.'

'That's enough of that,' Sam said: 'The horse probably won't survive. It's obviously an old horse someone's thrown out; it's no use planning things that won't come off.'

The horse turned his head from one to another, his ears moving, as if trying to make out the words.

'He's a lucky horse, an omen,' Debbie said.

Sam frowned at her. There was no such thing as magic. God ruled the world; and surely he had not sent them a horse, knowing how desperately hard up they were and how badly things were going. They needed a horse as much as they needed snow at strawberry time.

Debbie turned away, her shoulders humped, and Sam

cursed himself. He could do no right with this child of his, and he only wanted her own good. Maybe the horse was an omen, a talisman, as she said, and with his coming life would improve. And then he felt guilty because that was rank superstition.

Debbie was talking to Bob, her eyes eager, asking about the local shows and what kind of jumps. Sam had never allowed her to go to anything like them; it was wicked. She wished passionately she had been born into an ordinary family and could go off, like the girls at school, to the agricultural fair, could ride her horse and win, jumping each obstacle faultlessly. Sometimes she slipped away to watch the local children at the pony club practise their jumps in the riding-school field. She borrowed pony magazines from the girls at school. She would love to soar in the air as they soared. She could imagine the feeling. If only she could learn to jump.

She had been sent this horse, from the sea, a miracle horse, a miracle just for her. There were miracles, even in the Bible. Surely her father could see this horse had come to them for a purpose? The more she thought about it the more certain she was.

Sam looked at the horse and the horse looked back, its eyes holding his, almost as if it could read his thoughts. It began to tug at the haynet, ignoring the man. It certainly showed signs of improvement. Maybe if they could get it fit they could sell it; if it was a good horse, it would help meet those bills. Sam had put them on the dresser, reluctant to open any of them. Electricity; rates; oil for the greenhouses and heaven alone knew how much that would be; and also an income tax demand and the phone bill.

It never rained but it poured. He would have to open the letters; tot up the cost and go to the bank and see if they would increase his overdraft, and it wasn't that easy. But at least he had a good crop.

The telephone rang and he went indoors.

It was a London flower shop, wanting everything he had ready, for a big Society wedding. Their regular supplier had had his nursery wrecked by vandals the night before. Could he get the flowers on the early morning train? He couldn't, but he would, even if they had to pick by the lights of the Land-Rover and bunch all night. Debbie would have to help him. Sam knew that flower shop. They paid their bills promptly, which was more than many did; and it meant some money in the bank. Perhaps their luck was changing. He pushed the thought irritably out of his head, and picked up the bills.

It needed to change. More than £200 in back tax for last year; he had thought he was paid up to date, but they were always behind with those who worked for themselves. He looked at the oil bill; he knew oil had gone up but surely to goodness not like that? He worked it out. Five hundred gallons at 30 pence a gallon. One hundred and fifty pounds. It was correct. And he couldn't cut the heat off from the greenhouses, or they'd lose even more money. The electricity bill was over sixty pounds. And the telephone bill was nearly a hundred pounds; but he couldn't do business without it. Flower shops weren't open in the evenings. So he couldn't phone at cheap rates. He added it up. Over five hundred pounds. How was a man supposed to live? He felt so sick that even the big order failed to change his mood.

But business was business and the order had to be picked and packed and taken to the station. He went out into the yard.

'I've got the biggest order we've ever had,' he said to Debbie, who was watching the horse eat as if she had never seen an animal before. 'We'll have to pick and pack for half the night.'

'I'll put straw down for Blaze and then come and help.' She was feeling happier. The horse was on his feet and he was feeding. Bob had not the heart to tell her that he thought the horse was breathing badly and also had a temperature. Maybe if he helped out he could talk to Sam and make him change his mind about getting the veterinary help that the animal needed.

'Can I help too?' he asked. 'I've nothing to do and I'm bored to death. My horse is lame so I can't even ride, and dad's extra busy today. Mum's had to go to the hospital for treatment.' Debbie knew that Bob's mother spent all her waking time in a wheelchair. She was a brisk laughing woman who didn't seem to let whatever disability she had spoil life for those around her. She worked in the house and cooked like an angel.

'I'll be glad of help,' Sam said.

It was harder work than Bob had realised. They worked in silence; no time to talk. Pick too fast and the delicate stems broke; walk carelessly and you trod on the flowers. It was late March. There were daffodils and narcissi and tulips; there were iris in the greenhouse. There were freesia and anemones. Bob's back ached and his legs ached and the stems were surprisingly hard on the hands. He and Sam picked and Debbie bunched and put the bunches in baskets and carried them up to the house, ready to pack in the boxes.

Every time she went up to the house she looked in at the stable. She tried to fasten the blankets more tightly round Blaze. She had named him, and he belonged to her. He was shivering still. She fetched a third blanket from her own bed, and blocked up some of the worst holes in the stable walls. If only they had somewhere warmer for him.

Bob wanted to ask about the horse; he wanted to talk to Sam, but Sam was picking swiftly, expertly, grim-faced, figures dancing in front of his eyes. They would have to sell up. He couldn't keep on like this. He would be bankrupt if oil went up again. It was a good job they had chickens and eggs; and he grew salad in the greenhouses, in a corner, just for the two of them, as well as fruit and vegetables. They would have to live on their hump. There wasn't much hump left.

Sam eased his back and switched on the lights of the Land-Rover. Bob had forgotten that his parents had no idea where he was. He watched Debbie, her scarf slipping off her hair, her ugly clothes hampering her as she worked. She'd be much more comfortable in trousers and anorak, but she was wearing a too-long heavy tweed skirt and a thick jersey, and a flapping navy blue coat, and wellingtons. She moved so slowly she appeared to be sleepwalking. Bob had never appreciated how hard she and her father must have to work. And no one to cook for them. And he knew Debbie had been very ill indeed. Debbie had no idea that she had only escaped death herself. Sam knew.

Sam bent down to the flowers again. His back ached and

his hands were sore, but he could work without sleep if it meant some money in the bank; something to pay off that dreadful bunch of bills that had all come together and conspired to wreck him.

Debbie listened to the waves, pounding against the rocks far below them. It was difficult to believe the horse had been thrown against those same rocks; that they had pushed and heaved him all the way up the cliff, that he now stood in their stable, feeding occasionally, and raised his head to look at her when she came in. Her horse. The horse she had dreamed about for all those years, keeping her daydreams from her father as she grew up, knowing he thought them the silly prattle of a child and that he didn't realise the passion with which she yearned to have a horse of her own; a horse to fill the gap made by being without a mother. Sam could never have understood. She needed something to look after, something that was completely hers.

When Blaze was fit, she would ride him.

She bunched more flowers, working automatically, longing for bed. She passed the stable and heard the rustling in the straw and could not resist another look. The wise head looked at her; the long ears moved towards her as she spoke; she lifted her hand to stroke the muzzle and he unexpectedly dropped his huge tongue into her palm. She stared at it.

'Try squeezing it,' Bob suggested, coming up behind her to have another look himself. 'Someone's taught him that.'

Debbie squeezed. The horse bent his head and rubbed it against her cheek, grateful for attention, and for the comfort he had been given. It was nothing like the comfort he had had in Ireland; the well-built, draught-proof loose box, the deep shavings, the thick blanket; but it was a thousand times better than the rough sea and the rocky beach.

'Isn't he perfect?' Debbie asked Bob. He nodded, but his eyes were looking over the horse. He often went out with his father on his rounds and was studying to be a vet himself. He had already completed one year of his course. This was a very sick horse indeed. Bob swore inwardly. Of all people, it would have to land up in Sam's hands. None of Sam's animals ever came for attention.

62

Luckily they seemed extremely fit. Mop was a picture of health. The shaggy little dog was in the corner of the stable, admiring the horse, to which he had suddenly and completely given his loyalty. He didn't even follow Debbie indoors.

There were still boxes to pack and labels to write. Bob looked at the clock and realised his parents would be worrying. He asked Sam if he might phone and tell them where he was, and why he would like to stay on.

'I'll come over and help,' Michael Pope said at once. He was curious to see the horse that Johnnie had told him about that morning. Perhaps he could persuade Sam; this would be a natural way to introduce himself; a neighbourly helping-out. He had asked Bob about the horse and had received a guarded reply that told him something was very wrong. Sam was edgy about being helped, but he seemed in desperate need of assistance.

The vet appeared twenty minutes later, and sat down at the table to write labels for the boxes, while Sam and Debbie boxed the flowers quickly and expertly. Debbie was almost asleep. It was after midnight.

'It's cold outside,' Michael Pope said. 'Frost tonight.'

Sam stared at him. Frost was all he needed. He thought of the ranks of flowers. Late frost was the very devil. It was a brilliant night; clear sky, sharp stars, the moon gilding the sea. The worst kind of night for him. He swallowed, and said nothing. There was nothing he could say.

At last they were finished, and Debbie crawled wearily to bed, while Bob promised to look in on the horse. His father followed him. Sam was busy with the boxes, stacking them into the Land-Rover ready for the morning.

Michael Pope had noted the farmhouse; the bare room with trestles where they packed the flowers; the comfortable shabby kitchen, which Debbie had brightened with gay cheap cushion covers and curtains. She had taken over for her father in the last year, a wise competent child, too old for her age, treated as an adult, with never a moment for play. Her father often forgot that she was not yet fifteen.

Michael Pope shone his torch into the stable.

'Trouble,' he said softly. 'Do you think I could give him a sneaky injection?'

'He'll be better in the morning,' Sam said from behind them, and the vet felt guilty, lest he had been overheard. Sam watched Bob mount his bicycle and his father climb into the estate car, and then stumped off to bed.

He slept badly and woke early, at the first glimpse of dawn. Frost was white on the grass; frost was white on the trees; frost was white on the fence. He opened one of the boxes and checked it and sighed with relief. He'd been a fool to put them in the car, but at least the packed flowers were safe. He didn't deserve it, but he'd got away with it this time. He did not need to look at the fields. The greenhouses would be unharmed. But the outdoor crop . . .

He did not look at the horse.

Debbie woke an hour later and crawled out of bed, almost too stiff to move. She ached from picking, from stooping, from bunching; she ached from tiredness, but she had a horse now. She washed and dressed and made toast and coffee fast, and went outside to the stable just as Sam drove back from the station.

She opened the stable door.

The horse was standing with drooping head. Nose and eyes streamed with mucous and he coughed as she opened the door. He would not touch the mash she had made for him.

'He's dying,' Debbie said.

Sam said nothing. He had glanced across the fields and seen the stricken flowers and felt too sick for speech.

'He needs the vet,' Debbie said.

Still Sam said nothing. His face was grey. He was cold; so cold he wondered if he would ever be warm again. He had lost his crop and had bills to pay, and it was the end of everything he had worked for all these years. And what else could he do?

'God sent him from the sea,' Debbie shouted suddenly. 'God saved his life and sent him to us. Do you think God stops people having a vet? He doesn't. If you don't save him God will be angry and I'll hate you forever.'

It was more than Sam could bear.

Debbie was thumping him with her fists, tears streaming

down her face, semi-hysterical. He shook her roughly.

'Be quiet,' he said, in a soft voice that frightened her more than it would have done if he had shouted at her. 'We'll get the vet in. We'll get the horse absolutely fit and then we'll sell him. Maybe God sent him to us so that we could pay the bills.'

He walked away.

Debbie went into the stable and sat down on the edge of the manger. She would never speak to her father again.

The horse coughed and she went over to him and hid her face against his neck. It would be better if he died than if he were sold.

Either way, she couldn't bear it.

Michael Pope had been out early to a sick calf. He passed Sam's farm, and was tempted to go and look at the horse. But he needed to take things slowly. Sam couldn't be pushed. He might, just, be led.

'Sam Trelawny phoned,' Nancy, his wife, said. She wheeled her indoor chair to the table and began to dish the bacon and eggs and French toast. She had an electric wheelchair to get herself around the village. She liked being independent. 'He wants you to treat that horse.'

'What's got into Sam?' Michael asked.

'Maybe he's just coming to his senses,' Nancy said. 'Bob's gone over with one of our rugs so that they can fix him up properly. He said that poor pathetic child had tied on her own bed blankets with string.'

Michael Pope glanced at the clock. Just time to go over there before surgery. His surgeries were rarely busy; the village animals were a healthy crew and the country people knew what to do in most cases of sickness. It was just the accidents that kept him busy. Country boys were just as stupid about breaking milk bottles as were those in the town, though they got their ears clipped if Michael or Tim Marney, the local policeman, saw them. Village people were much more realistic about things than those who lived in cities.

Debbie was white-faced when Michael reached the stable. The horse drooped, his breath rasping horribly, and his body was racked with shivers.

'Don't hope too much, Debbie,' Michael said. 'Drugs work

wonders but they can't work miracles. He's a very sick horse indeed. He's had a terrible time before contracting this illness.' Michael didn't say that he should have been called days before.

'Dad wants to sell him when he's better, to pay the bills,' Debbie said. 'It doesn't matter if he doesn't get well . . . it . . .'

She ran out of the stable, along the cliff top and down the steps to the beach, away from everything and everyone, unable to face any of them. The waves thundering on the rocks, the gulls gliding through the sky, crying forlornly, the wind cold on her face, reflected her mood. If she walked out on to the rocks she could slide into the sea and drown and her father would be sorry he didn't let her keep the horse. Or he could sell it and get his money and without her he'd be rich. He was always grumbling about bills.

If her mother had been alive she would have made him let her keep the horse. Debbie couldn't remember her mother at all; she only knew her as a beautiful picture, in her bridal dress, laughing up at a much younger Sam who was laughing too. She daydreamed about her; inventing conversations that comforted her, as in them Debbie always got her own way.

Her mother would have wanted her to have the horse and to show-jump with him. Her mother would have got the vet and wouldn't have let Blaze be sold.

There were footsteps on the rocks.

'Come on, Debbie,' Bob said. 'We've got to make the stable draughtproof, or your horse won't survive. Your father can't sell him for months; he won't be fit, and by then anything might have happened.'

Debbie didn't believe him, but she went back to the stable to find that Mary and her father, the village policeman, who was off duty, were helping Jim Hannitance, who wasn't quite all there, to stack bales of straw around the stable, to insulate the walls against the draughts.

'Dad borrowed the straw bales,' Bob said. 'They're as safe here as they were in old Len Idle's barn; and doing much more good. Jim's going to put two tarpaulins over the roof and by then we should have Blaze as snug as if he were in a racing stable, without a whisper of a draught anywhere.'

It was something to do; something to take her mind off the horse's condition. Blaze watched them apathetically as they stacked the bales, making sure they were safe and couldn't fall. There was a wall of straw all round him soon. Bob piled straw thick under his hooves, till he stood deep in the litter it made. Jim had cleared the soiled bedding out before Debbie came.

'He's feeling better already,' Bob said, stroking his smooth neck. 'He's stopped shivering.'

The thick horse blanket was finally secured, with a second rug on top of it. Debbie brought clean water, and the horse drank, very briefly, and blew at her half-heartedly. She sponged the scummy eyes and nose again.

'He looks so ill,' Debbie said forlornly.

'Time works wonders,' Michael Pope said, coming back into the stable. He had been talking to Sam, who was bewildered by the sudden interest in him, not knowing that Michael Pope had driven past the blighted fields in the early morning on his way to a sick cow, and had put two and two swiftly together, and alerted the village. Everyone was ready to help.

'Time for surgery,' Nancy Pope said, propelling her electric chair into the yard. Mop barked, as much at the accompanying Alsatian and wolfhound as at the chair. 'I'll stay here for a bit. I need a change. I'm tired of our four walls.'

Bob stared at his mother. She never was inside their own four walls. She managed to be down on one farm, bottle-feeding baby lambs, on another helping to rear motherless piglets, over at a dog breeder's where she played with the pups. If she were at home, she was usually nursing one animal or another that had been brought to them to be looked after.

Nancy signalled to him swiftly, with a quick wink, and the penny dropped. Debbie, who had never met Bob's mother, though she had often seen her, stood looking at Nancy, not knowing quite what to say. It must be awful to be unable to walk. Nancy had been crippled in a bad car crash some years ago.

'We'll get your horse right, pet,' Nancy said. 'Meanwhile let the men get on with putting the stable right, and what about a meal for you and your father? I've brought a casserole with me; I thought you'd be too busy to cook. Michael tells me that the frost got all the flowers in the fields. Maybe you can pick the greenhouse orders and I can bunch the flowers while your father does whatever's necessary with the spoiled crops. This will sit in the oven and heat through by lunch time. There's enough for an army.'

Debbie stared at her. She hadn't even looked at the fields. No wonder Sam had been so angry with her. She had only thought of the horse. She walked down the path beyond the hedge and stared at the devastation. Sam saw her and came over.

'It's bad, Debbie,' he said. 'We've nothing at all left of the outdoor crops.'

'One thing,' Nancy Pope said, coming up to them, as the path was wide enough for the wheelchair. 'Everyone will have been hit alike and your greenhouses are full. The price of those indoor flowers will soar. Not a total loss.'

'I hadn't thought of that,' Sam said.

He walked back to the greenhouses. Come day, go day, there were flowers to water, flowers to pick and orders to pack, and he would have to make plans for those ruined fields and recoup his losses somehow.

Michael Pope was waiting for him at lunch time, having come back to look at the horse. Nancy's casserole was ready to eat. Sam had carried her into the house and put her in an easy chair beside the fire, while Debbie dished up the food. She added another plate for Michael

'There's a small improvement,' Michael Pope said. 'If I get this horse right, my reputation will go sky high. Everyone in Cornwall will be talking about it. Nancy can help Debbie with the nursing, and Bob will come over and watch at nights; and we'll make history. The horse that came from the sea, and Michael Pope, the vet that worked a miracle. I'll be as famous as James Herriot without the need to write all those books.'

He grinned suddenly at Debbie.

'Don't look so tragic, love. I've a feeling your horse will be all right.'

'How much do you think he'll fetch when he's fit?' Sam asked, avoiding Debbie's eyes. The bills were behind him on the dresser, and he could see them tormenting him, without even turning his head. If the horse were a good one, as Michael Pope said, maybe he could sell it for a thousand pounds.

'He won't be fit for months; not fit enough to sell,' Michael Pope said, and saw the relief on Debbie's face.

'And how much will he cost to treat?' Sam asked grimly, coming at last to the really vital question. Treatment didn't come free.

'I've just said,' Michael Pope replied. 'I want the credit for curing him; and that's worth much more than the cost of his treatment to me.'

Sam stood up violently, overturning his chair. Debbie watched him, white-faced. Her father got angry so fast these days.

'I'll take no charity,' Sam said. 'Everyone coming round here with offers of help and with straw on loan and with food as if we were paupers; we've managed since my wife died and we'll go on managing. I'll pay for what I have.'

'I don't know if your damned horse will live, or die.' Michael Pope shouted back, beyond all patience. 'I told you I want to try; I don't know if the treatment will work; I've never had a sick horse that's been so exhausted before. If I can work out a cure it will help all sorts of people; especially the race-horse breeders. A horse that's run in a race can be as exhausted and then if he gets ill . . . pow! He's a very sick horse indeed. I want experience; and you can let me have it. There's no charity involved. And I'm not letting a lovely animal die because of your insane beliefs. I'll get the RSPCA if you won't co-operate.'

Sam sat down, aware of Nancy's eyes on him, considering. Aware also that he had frightened Debbie; that his temper was in shreds, and there was too much to worry about and he was exhausted. So exhausted that he didn't know how he would get through the day.

The telephone rang and Bob answered it.

'Flowers wanted,' he said and Sam took the phone, making notes on a pad. 'Yes, I've got them in the greenhouses,' he said. He rang off, and looked at the rest of them.

'There's a shortage of flowers,' he said. 'And my greenhouses are full, and I've got a head start. I'd best be picking.'

69

Michael Pope stood up too.

'I've got the farms to visit,' he said. 'Bob can help pick. He's nothing to do till term begins at college. He's at Liverpool. He's been helping me with the practice, but he'll see that horse in all sorts of conditions that he wouldn't see if he only came with me to treat him and he will know if anything else is needed to tide him over if there is an emergency. The horse isn't out of the wood yet.'

He left, and Debbie and Bob carried the plates into the scullery and then went out of the back door to look at Blaze. Sam stood frowning, wondering if he ought to help Nancy back into her wheelchair or if she would interpret that as a suggestion that she should go.

'Sam,' Nancy said. 'I've work to do and I can't make that chair on my own.' She smiled at him. 'People need people. I couldn't manage if folk didn't rally round; no one is offering you charity. I tried to be independent – it doesn't work and it isn't fair to others. You really will help Michael by letting him treat that horse. The horse doesn't share your beliefs. And he's an owner somewhere. He's entitled to every chance that you and Michael can give him. You could help me by letting me borrow Debbie sometimes. There are things she could do for me that the men are bad at, like washing my hair. I have a girl come from town to do it but it's expensive. And I haven't a daughter. I don't often get the chance to talk woman-talk. I could teach her to sew too, and to knit. And there are all the clothes I'll never wear again because I've put on so much weight in this damned chair. Trousers and jerseys and blouses that don't fit me and that I've refused to give away in case one day I miraculously walk again. Well, I'm not going to and that's that. I've come to terms with it; Debbie could help me a lot by coming in and out. I miss Bob when he's away.'

Sam lifted her gently, saying nothing. He settled Nancy and pulled the rug round her. The two dogs were lying patiently, waiting. Their tails thumped as Sam carried their mistress outside.

'It took a long time to accept any help at all,' Nancy said. 'I've got my pride too. And then I realised that I can still do my share; the people around help when I need it and I can help them; I can bake and I can mend, and I can look after small children and help out with their animals when they are sick. Who was it said "No man's an island"? It's true, Sam. One day, you'll return everything that's been done to help you; so who's the loser?'

'I've been used to managing,' Sam said.

'It's not much fun, just managing,' Nancy said, patting the wolfhound's cold nose, which he had thrust into her hand.

'Man was born to trouble as the sparks fly upwards,' Sam said.

'I don't believe that,' Nancy said passionately. 'Look at this place; at the cliffs and the sea and the flowers in the greenhouses; at the sky and the trees and the sun on the horizon. It's beautiful and was meant to be enjoyed. Being alive isn't a penance, Sam. I nearly died, you know. Every day's a gift, to make the most of.' Nancy laughed. 'I sound like a preacher or something. Come on, Sam. Relax a bit and let Debbie have a little fun. It won't make her bad; it will do her the world of good. Let her keep her horse. You'll manage somehow.'

Sam's face was grim.

'That would be madness,' he said. 'As soon as the horse is fit, he'll have to be sold. I'm not changing my mind about that.'

Debbie, coming round the corner of the path, stood quite still and watched her father walk away. Nancy could not read the expression in the blue eyes. She had never seen such a look on any child's face. When she got to bed that night it worried her so much that it prevented her from sleeping. Whenever she closed her eyes she saw again the set jaw and the implacable accusation in the eyes.

Sam was on a one-way ride to disaster, that was for sure.

Chapter Seven

Nancy Pope had a genius for collecting strays; Shane, her wolfhound, had been abandoned on a motorway, probably because he was big and boisterous and cost so much to feed. Rebel, the Alsatian, had been brought to be put down because he had been jealous of a new baby. He gave all his allegiance to Nancy. And now she added Debbie to her collection, almost casually fulfilling both her own need for a daughter and Debbie's for a mother. There had never been a woman in Debbie's life.

Nancy, talking to the child as they watched over the horse, realised that Debbie was growing up fast and asking questions that would astonish Sam if he knew them. She dared not ask her father. She did not see why she should be different from her friends; should go around in ugly clothes with her hair covered; should never cut her hair or wear make-up when she was older.

And she needed to earn money for her horse. Somehow, she would pay for all his food. Blaze had been sent to her for a purpose. Sam said that God worked in mysterious ways and this was one of them.

Slowly, the next three weeks went by. Sam did not even realise that his daughter was not speaking to him. She cooked his meals, ate her own before him, swiftly, and then went out to Sam, saying merely that food was on the table. She spent her time with the horse; sometimes helping with the flowers, doing the necessary household chores, planning ceaselessly how she could earn money and pay for Blaze's food and bedding. He wouldn't be able to sleep in the fields, or go outside in all weathers for a very long time.

The horse was improving. The injections were working, and his temperature had fallen. He was still coughing and it was necessary to keep him very warm and treat the cough. He watched constantly for Debbie, as she meant comfort;

the crusted matter was sponged away from his eyes and nostrils, and he was groomed, and rugged again swiftly and fed warm mashes in tiny quantities. Little and often, Michael Pope said, watching over his patient with an expert eye, delighted to see him improve. Bob came daily too, and helped Sam, realising that Debbie preferred to be in the stable, looking after her patient.

Twice he pushed his mother down the lane in her outdoor wheelchair, so that they could entice Debbie for a change of scene and a meal. Bob deliberately left early and there was no one else to push Nancy home. Debbie loved the vet's house; big, roomy, old and shabby, with comfortable chairs and log fires, and animals everywhere. A Siamese cat and her kittens dominated the hearthrug; the dogs lay quietly on their own rugs in the corners of the room, out of the way. Shane was enormous. A big tabby with only one eye shared his rug. The kittens preferred Rebel's and clambered over the dog, who bore their needlelike claws patiently, shaking them off when he was tired of them. Their mother was less patient. They were weaned but refused to accept the fact and when they tried to nurse she boxed their ears.

There was always so much laughter in the house. Sam never laughed. Nancy looked out her useless clothes from her wardrobe; slim-fitting trousers and jerseys that she had not wanted to part with, sure that one day she would walk again and be elegant again. One day wasn't going to come. She gave them to Debbie, who tried them on in the bedroom, looking at herself in the mirror, unable to believe in what she saw. There were no mirrors at home. She looked taller, and slender, and more like the other girls at school . . . She brushed out her long fair hair. It slid over her shoulders in a gleaming sheaf.

Nancy looked at the girl as she came back into the room. Sam was going to have a headache before very long and maybe she shouldn't interfere. But she knew that Debbie would rebel, as soon as she was old enough. Better to let her get used to living in the world as it was. Sam couldn't lock her away for ever. And rebellion at eighteen might well be a disaster. This way was surely innocent enough.

Debbie didn't want to change back into the ugly clothes Sam chose for her. She was sitting cross-legged on the hearthrug laughing at the kittens, when Michael Pope came into the room. He glanced at her, and looked again, then looked at his wife, who put a finger on her lips. He had never imagined such a transformation.

'Blaze is going to be all right,' Michael said.

'He's not well enough to sell?' Debbie's expression had changed completely. He looked down at her terrified face.

'Not for months, Debbie,' he reassured her. 'He's not worth anything just now; he needs a great deal of careful nursing and then we'll have to work on him to get him fit. That will take at least a year, after a pasting like he's had. I'd love to know his history. The horse that came out of the sea. It sounds like a fairy story.'

'It doesn't feel like one,' Debbie said. She had been relaxed, enjoying talking to Nancy about clothes, and about a programme on wild life they had just watched together on television. Bob was up with Sam, helping to remedy the damage done by the frost.

'I must go,' Debbie said reluctantly. She went out of the room and changed into her skirt and jersey and pulled her hair into the two ruthless pigtails that Sam insisted on. The plaits were heavy and made her head ache. She looked wistfully at Nancy's short cropped hair; it must be lovely to be so free.

She picked up the smallest kitten and held it against her face, and then said good-bye, walking as if she were going to her execution.

'I can't bear to see that child like that,' Nancy said angrily, as her husband poured himself a whisky, added a squirt of soda, and then brought her a glass too.

'I don't like interfering,' Michael Pope said. 'But I couldn't let that horse die.'

'Debbie's more important than the horse,' Nancy said passionately. 'Look at the life she leads; she's a slave in that house. She'd be better off going back to school, whatever the doctor says. The fresh air may be good for her, but all that work! They never stop, either of them, and Sam's religion is warping life for both of them. He's a fanatic.'

'I'm not sure about that,' Michael Pope said. 'He's not consistent. I suspect he has doubts and is all the more rigid with Debbie because he's afraid to admit them.' Two kittens had settled on the vet's knee and a third on his shoulder. Evening surgery was over, and for once there were no emergencies. Firelight played on the walls. Nancy, sitting in her favourite chair, felt renewed, and pretended that she could walk again and in a few moments would get up and cross the room and tidy up the table. The wheelchair was out of sight, in the hall.

'Do you remember how I felt when I knew I'd never walk again?' Nancy asked.

'As if I could forget,' Michael Pope said.

'I hated you all; and the man who had crashed into my car; I hated living. But you and Bob were there for me, and helped. Sam has never had anyone to help him out of his misery. He's struggled on his own and become bitter.'

'And how does he change?' Michael Pope asked.

'Debbie will change him. I don't know whether for better, or worse. She'll rebel; she may leave him altogether. She's near breaking point already. If he sells that horse, God knows what she'll do. She's a very determined child.' Nancy stroked the wolfhound's head. He had come to lie against her chair and looked up at her, anxious to be noticed.

'And you're encouraging her,' Michael Pope said, more as a question than a statement.

'No. I'm trying to get her to trust me, and if she rebels to do it gradually, under my eyes and with my guidance,' Nancy said. 'Slowly, over a period, not in one terrible blast. She's nearly fifteen, Michael, and she's old for her age; and she's never done any of the things normal girls do. Supposing she falls in love with the wrong sort of person? She'll go head over heels into a world of experience she's not prepared for. Sam has sheltered her all her life.'

'It's not our problem,' Michael Pope said slowly. His wife looked at him, and he knew that they had added yet one more waif to their care. Nancy should have had an enormous family, he thought irrelevantly, and picked her up to carry her to bed. Debbie had turned the bed down and laid out Nancy's night clothes and there beside them on the pillow was a tiny posy of spring flowers, beautifully arranged, a ribbon tying the stems.

Nancy looked at it.

'Do you still think I can stay uninvolved?' she asked.

Bob was just leaving as Debbie arrived home.

'I've seen to Blaze for you,' he called, over his shoulder. 'He's tons better. He's got clean straw and had his evening meal.'

Debbie went into the stable. The long tongue dropped into her hand and as she squeezed it, the horse laid his cheek against hers, his head resting on her shoulder. She put her arms round his neck. No one was going to sell him.

Sam was doing his accounts when she went indoors. She knew better than to disturb him. She made a drink for both of them, and put the parcel of clothes that Nancy had given her down on the chair, hoping he might ask her about it. He said nothing. The figures were still frightening, although the bank manager had promised a loan to tide him over. There was the interest on that too.

'Blaze needs more food,' Debbie said, in a tight-controlled voice, after looking in the feed store. 'There's only enough for tomorrow. Please may I have some money for him?'

Sam glared at her.

'He costs far too much; I wish we'd never found him,' he said angrily, but he put a five-pound note on the table. Debbie took it, and made up her mind to pay it back immediately, without knowing how. The school term had ended; there were three weeks of holiday and the doctor had said she could go back next term. She didn't feel well enough to go back, ever. She wanted to stay with the horse, to laze in the sunshine. Bob would return to college. She would miss him too.

'There are ten posies and ten buttonholes to make before you go to bed,' Sam said. 'I expected you back long ago. Bob can pick flowers. Neither he nor I can arrange them. There's a wedding in Mevagissey tomorrow. He's taking the flowers over for me.'

'If I go with him I can get Blaze's food,' Debbie said.

She settled herself at the table with wire and scissors and ribbons. She felt so exhausted but it was her own fault for staying so long with Nancy. It was heaven to sit in front of the fire and do nothing but play with the kittens. Nancy had given her some hand cream. Her hands were so sore. Nearly raw, with the picking, with the water, and the wind. Flowers were almost more demanding than horses.

She slipped out into the yard before going to bed. The ten posies and the buttonholes were ready. It was nearly one o'clock. Sam put them in the refrigerator. They would be fresh in the morning. Blaze was standing in the straw. His eager head turned to her when she opened the half door. She looked up into his eyes and he huffed at her. She blew gently into his nostrils, exchanging thoughts silently, communicating with him wordlessly. The horse knew how much she cherished him, and she had no need to be told that she was the most important creature in his life now, whatever his past had been.

Bob arrived early in the morning, driving the little Mini that his father kept to use when the estate car was being serviced or repaired. Debbie had put on Nancy's blue trousers and a white jersey. Her hair was loose. She slipped quickly out of the house before Sam noticed. He saw her from the back as she got into the car and thought Bob had brought another passenger. He checked the refrigerator and the table. All the flower boxes had gone.

Debbie, free for the day, was a different person, laughing and talking eagerly about the horse, and all she intended to do with him, as they drove. The flowers were delivered, the horse food was bought and then Bob had some shopping to do for his mother. Debbie, wandering along the little high street, saw an advertisement in the hairdresser's window and stared at it.

£5 for real hair.

She went inside and came out twenty minutes later with her hair cropped like Nancy's, a soft cap of shining pale gold; the two plaits had been exchanged for a five-pound note. She had the money for Blaze's feed for the next few days. Maybe she could find work and get paid for it; she joined Bob in the car park and he stared at her.

'What on earth will your father say?'

'I don't know,' Debbie said. She suddenly did know and her inside was a hard knot of misery so that it was all she could do to drink the cup of coffee Bob bought for her before they went home. This time she did not talk at all. She knew she had to face Sam; face him with short hair uncovered and wearing Nancy's slacks and jersey. There was a hooded

77

coat on the back seat, a frivolous coat with a scarlet lining, that Nancy had loved.

'Shall I come with you?' Bob asked, drawing up in the yard. Debbie shook her head. She had to face this alone. She not only had the money for her hair, but the flower shop had paid cash for the posies. The money was in an envelope. Perhaps that would sweeten her father. He only seemed to think of money these days. She had no idea of the size of their bills or the cost of running the place.

She went into the stable to Blaze, to gain courage to walk through the fields to the cliff top where she knew Sam would be busy planting out. It was a beautiful day, the sun shining and the air warm. She put a halter on the horse and led him into the yard. He stood looking about him and then followed Debbie into the lane. She led him for a few yards. It was his first venture from the stable. He moved slowly, and Mop followed. The little dog now never left the horse. He slept in the stable, or lay across the stable door outside in the yard. He had completely broken his allegiance to Debbie.

Blaze watched for Mop coming. He hated aloneness. The dog was company.

Sam, coming up from the field, saw a slender girl in blue slacks and a close-fitting jersey leading a horse down the lane. Her fair hair gleamed in the sun. He frowned, wondering what she was doing there. He recognised the horse before he recognised Debbie. He stood quite still, staring at her speechless.

Debbie said nothing. She held out the envelope from the shop with the money in it, and her own five-pound note, and walked straight past Sam into the stable, where she took the halter off the horse, and eased the rug.

Sam walked into the kitchen. The brightly-lined hooded coat lay on the chair. He made coffee for both of them, for the moment unable to face the situation at all. There was a letter on the table, in Debbie's handwriting, the envelope addressed to her grandmother, his dead wife's mother. He wondered why she was writing again. She had posted her weekly letter the day before.

Debbie walked into the room. She had summoned up all the courage she had.

'I've written to Gran,' she said. 'She's got a stable for Blaze and she's always said I can go and live with her whenever I want. I'm tired of ugly clothes and church every Sunday and people who make me feel as if I'm wicked all the time. It isn't wrong to wear pretty clothes; other girls do and they don't drop dead. It isn't wrong to like pretty things; God made them too; flowers, and kittens; I hate the way we live. You grumbled when I made the cushion covers; everything your Church talks about makes the world a horrible place; a cruel place, where it's wrong to enjoy being alive. I hate it; I hate living here and working all the time and never going anywhere else; and no one is going to take Blaze from me. Not you, not anyone. If Gran won't have me I'll run away.'

'You're talking nonsense,' Sam said. 'Get changed into your decent clothes and have some sense. And what do you imagine you've done with your hair? You know perfectly well I won't have you looking like those young flibbertigibbets with no religion.'

'I don't see why we have to be so different,' Debbie said passionately. 'It's not a religion. It's wicked. At school they say a prayer to beauty; thank God for all that is wonderful in this world; the stars and the night sky; the sun and the bright day; the birds and the flowers and the trees, and for the privilege of life. All your Church ever talks about is hell fire and sin and burning. I'm not going any more. Ever.'

She turned and walked out of the room, slamming the door to hide the sobs that she couldn't stifle. She hadn't known she had so much courage, nor had she ever realised before quite what she thought.

In the kitchen Sam sat with his coffee in front of him, staring at the letter she had written. He could not think. He threw the cold liquid down the sink, rinsed the cup and went out into the yard. The horse had his head over the door. He saw Sam, and neighed a welcome.

Sam walked over and stroked the animal. Blaze was no longer sick. He had begun to look well again. His coat was developing a gleam and his eyes were bright.

Sam stood beside the animal, lost in thought. He couldn't keep the horse. He shouldn't let Debbie get away with her rebellion. They hadn't the money, and the whole thing was absurd. The sun beat down on his head. Nini rolled on the cobbles, her small black body stretched sensuously full length to bask in the spring warmth. The sea was a gentle murmur, seducing him from work. Debbie was so like his wife that it was uncanny.

His mind went back to those first days of marriage. He had rebelled against his stepfather's stern religious principles; had married outside his wishes. He had always felt he had been punished for his sin. His stepfather had made his doubts certain; emphasising over and over what happened to unbelievers, to lambs who strayed from the fold. He had been a great one for triteness, had the old man. Sam could see the stern face, the white beard, the piercing black eyes, could hear the deep angry voice, the sarcasm that had lacerated him so often as a child.

Was he doing that to Debbie?

He had forgotten how it felt to be fifteen, but he remembered, vividly, his own rebellion at twenty-two; the runaway marriage; aided and abetted by Elizabeth's mother who had always hated his stepfather's stark version of religion. She had kept in touch with Debbie, had wanted the child, but Sam had refused to part with her. He knew that Debbie would be trebly welcome now.

The horse nudged his shoulder, impatient, wanting food. It was time for food, and Debbie was crying on her bed and Sam was lost in his own misery. The movement reminded him of earlier childhood, of his own pony, all those years ago, before his real father died. Life had been all laughter then; they had all been passionate about horses. His pony had been black, a delicately-made little creature named Soot, most unoriginally. His mother had laughed at him, but he had been an unoriginal child.

Debbie had generations of horse owners in her blood; and so had he. He went in to make the mash.

The coat had gone, and so had the letter. He ran upstairs, but Debbie's room was empty. She had taken nothing with her; he looked in the drawers and in the wardrobe. But he did not know what Nancy had given her. He ran outside, and the horse neighed again, but Sam did not hear it. He was sure that Debbie had left him. She had gone to her grandmother, and he was alone. She would send for the horse.

He might catch her before she reached the station. He jumped into the Land-Rover and drove out of the yard.

Debbie crept out of hiding.

She put a halter on the horse, and led him into the lane. She didn't know where she was going. She would find somewhere to hide; all the farms had huge barns, and she could shift from one to another, somehow. She hadn't thought it out. She had only known, lying on her bed, that she couldn't stand any of it any more. She was going to her grandmother, even if she had to walk. Her father wouldn't give her the fares and she had no money of her own.

And when she went back to school she wouldn't be able to watch over the horse. He could be sold and away in a horse box as soon as she had taken the bus, and by the end of the day be out of her reach goodness knew where, and perhaps not looked after properly, or sold to drag a cart, or worse, for horse meat.

Sam wouldn't miss her. Except for picking flowers. He didn't care. All he cared about was money and being a saint in a hair shirt, like the saints they read about at school. She couldn't be a saint and wasn't going to try. Bob's mother was pretty and wore pretty things, and it wasn't wicked.

Debbie trudged along the lane, the horse beside her, her thoughts going over and over the same path, uselessly. She turned off on to the cliffs. She needed to plan. It was a long way to Sussex where her grandmother lived and Blaze wasn't fit. He couldn't make the journey. He was already starving, and once he stumbled.

She would have to go back.

Below her the sea murmured ceaselessly. She dropped on to the grass, too tormented to think, and the horse cropped the turf idly. He was enjoying the sunshine and the freedom, away from the stable.

At the station, Sam sat in the Land-Rover, baffled. Debbie hadn't taken the train. No one had seen her. He drove to Michael Pope's. Nancy hadn't seen her either. Worry flared in both their faces.

'Suppose she's hitch-hiked?' Sam asked, despair in his

voice. Debbie knew nothing of the world and there were villains about.

Nancy wanted to shout at him, to tell him he had brought this on himself, that the life he gave the child wasn't a life for anyone; that Debbie needed freedom and the chance to grow up, and live her own life. But she couldn't say the words.

Sam drove back to the empty farmhouse. He could not work, though there were orders to fulfil. There was nothing he could do and he did not know where to look.

A nose nudged his ankle. Mop had run home, terrified by the thunder, unable to keep up with Blaze. Sam looked at the dog and whistled to him, to put him in the stable. He stared at the empty stall in disbelief.

Out on the cliffs Debbie slept, exhausted, unable to plan anything. She had tied Blaze to a tree and he stood beside her, placid. Far out at sea thunder clouds rolled together and there was a background of ominous sound. Sam, standing beside Mop in the stable yard, stared at the sky. Hail would be a disaster, and hail often came with thunder. And where was Debbie? Neither she nor the horse was a hundred per cent fit. If they were caught in the storm . . . At least she hadn't hitch-hiked. The child must be out of her mind.

Out on the cliffs, Debbie slept on, unaware of the change in the weather. Lightning ripped the sky. The birds were silent. Blaze moved uneasily and then, as the thunder rolled, he plunged, and the halter broke. Debbie woke to see him galloping over the grass, to see the sky dark and to feel the first hail hit against her skin. She would be soaked. And the horse would get drenched and be ill again.

She stumbled after him, trying to shield her face against the blinding stones that stung and bruised her, trying to shout above the sound of rain and wind and thunder, knowing there was danger on the cliffs; danger of subsidence; of the sudden slip and slide of the turf at the edge; of hidden gullies; of crumbling rocks; of a terrified horse plunging to the death he had escaped from once.

And it was all her fault. Her father's God was punishing her.

She ran on, the breath rasping in her lungs, her heart

pounding. The horse had vanished. He might never have been. She could neither see nor hear. She crouched under the overhang of a wall, away from trees, and listened to the pealing from the sky, on, and on, and on, while rain pelted down unceasingly, obscuring her view.

Chapter Eight

Jack Savage was something of a mystery to the villagers. He lived in a converted cottage that had once been a tied cottage on the big farm. This he had modernised. He had added a large stable with two stalls, and a storehouse for feed. The village children were afraid of the old man; he was daunting, with his erect figure, his severe face with the short white beard, always silky and beautifully trimmed; the white moustache and hair, and vivid blue eyes. He was shy with children, and never knew what to say, so that they assumed he hated them, and avoided him whenever possible.

He kept one hunter, a massive chestnut named Colonel; he also had a golden retriever, an elderly dog, as stately as his master, named Major, and a cat called Private Jones, a small personal joke that the old man could not share with anyone. Private Jones had been a grand fighter he had known in the Great War, a formidable boxer, and the cat was a warrior, one-eyed and fierce with any other cat that dared invade his territory.

The villagers knew the old man had once had to do with horses. They did not know that Jack Savage's father had been one of the most famous trainers of his day, and had bred a number of horses that men coveted as much as women coveted jewels. Jack Savage himself had grown up in the stables; had ridden his first race at the age of twelve, and gone on to become a leading jockey; had retired and taken up training and breeding, enjoying life between the wars, taking horses to race in Australia, in India, in Norway, in Sweden, in America, in France. He and his wife had been respected and admired in all racing circles. His wife had run the business side for him, expertly and with a flair for money that Jack had never had.

But age respected no one. Elspeth died, and Jack was alone, and he soon realised that he could not manage without her; nor was there any savour. His son took over the business, and paid the old man an income princely enough to let him keep his hunter and live well.

Jack did not want to be a ghost haunting his old home; he did not want to see things done that he would not have approved; nor to give unasked for advice. He had seen too much conflict between father and son, working together. He did not want pity. He moved as far away as possible and busied himself with his horse and his dog and his cat and his garden. He hunted, sedately, at the rear of the Hunt, avoiding the fences, knowing that if he fell and injured himself he would become a burden. He would never allow that.

He was lonely, but he allowed no one to even guess. He took a nightly drink with a few of the Hunt members, and nodded to them and went, not wishing to intrude; not to be asked home out of charity. 'The old boy's a bit of a bore, but he's on his own.' That he couldn't bear.

Mrs Pemberthy, who worked for him, tidied up the horse magazines, and told her friends about the signed pictures of great horses that hung all round his walls; portraits in oils; photographs of horses that had been by-words; there was a bronze statue of his most famous winner on the mantelpiece in the living-room, given him by the horse's owner when Jack retired. It was his most cherished possession after his animals.

Jack Savage had stabled his horse just before the storm started. Private Jones rushed in, aware of thunder in the air, and was curled on the hearthrug, a gleaming black mass upon the gold. Major was uneasy. Jack Savage suddenly realised it was probably because the horse was stamping in his stall. Colonel hated thunder. As the rumbles came nearer, the old man put on his raincoat, whistled the dog and went outside, to stand in the stall and gentle the chestnut in a way that had not changed since the first man tamed the first horse.

Jack Savage closed the half door, but could not bear the enclosed atmosphere in the stable and opened it again, just as lightning flashed over the sky. He stared. He had never seen anything like it in England. It was early in the year for storms, and this was spectacular. The flickering zig-zags raked through the air, again and again and again, lighting everywhere with brilliance that made the intervals between even more dark.

The dog crouched in the straw, leaning against Jack's leg. The horse was trembling, also leaning against the old man, whose fingers were reassuring on the long neck. Jack Savage moved to shut the half door again as rain poured down, and another flash lit up the sky, the thunder crashed almost simultaneous. He thought for one horrifying moment that the cottage had been hit.

Lightning flashed again and with it, over the hedge at the end of his garden came a horse, spread against the sky, leaping up and up, as if it had taken off for ever. Jack saw the stretched legs, the powerful neck, the flying hooves, the poised body; and then there was darkness.

He closed the stable door and ran outside.

Blaze had exhausted himself. The noise and the light had terrified him beyond reason and he had bolted, not knowing his direction. On and on, hunted by the devils that roared in the air, that blinded him with their weapons, that threw hailstones at him that stung his skin and hurt his eyes. He had run, head down, once putting his hoof into a rabbit burrow, once slipping and falling headlong and picking himself up again and racing on, away from the noise, away from the lashing rain, away from danger. He had known storms before, but only in the safety of his stable; only with Dan's reassuring voice to soothe him, and never a storm like this. Behind the rain came the wind, a roaring, bellowing, horrifying, unseen enemy that buffeted him, and beyond him the sea piled itself against the rocks, smashing against the unyielding land with a din of surf that was worse than all the other noises put together, ceaseless, unrelenting, threatening him.

He saw the hedge in front of him and rose to clear it, up and up, borne in panic that had reduced him to a bolting unreasoning animal, knowing nothing, more afraid than ever he had been in the sea. He landed in soft earth, shaken by the drop, his soaked sides heaving, his head down, all the energy gone from him, exhausted by the gallop and by that last immense leap.

Jack Savage held the image in his eye of the huge horse clearing the hedge that he had thought unjumpable. He went to the horse, and was overwhelmed by anger. The broken headrope showed carelessness; the lacerations were half healed; who in hell had let the animal escape in such condition on a day like this, in weather like this? This horse had been ill and wasn't yet recovered.

He led Blaze into the empty stall. He removed the soaked blanket, and put huge rough towels over the animal. He tedded straw underfoot; he turned on the big fan heater, to warm the air. He worked fast, regaining old skills, buoyed by fury. He would find out who owned the animal and he would have plenty to say. He did not usually interfere, but he would never see a horse, or any other defenceless creature, ill used.

Later he would ring the vet and find out who owned this horse. It must be someone local. Meanwhile he had work to do. He began to rub the saturated coat, humming to himself, to soothe Colonel in the next stall as well as this terrified beast that was shivering and panting as if it would never stop.

Debbie had run until she could run no more; she had sheltered from the hail, and then, when the rain eased and the wind died, she came out from the lee of the wall that had given her very little protection, soaked, and exhausted as much by misery as by the weather, and stumbled on, following the deep impressions left by Blaze's speeding hooves.

He had run for miles across the cliffs, but at least he had headed inland. She was not going home; she had to find him. He might have fallen and broken his neck, or jumped too high a fence and broken a leg; he might have burst a blood vessel. He must be terrified and she wasn't there. She felt sick at her own stupidity; sick at the thought of going home; sick at the knowledge that whatever happened, Blaze would be sold; and she would be left without him to endure the loneliness and the constant work and her father's stern religion that allowed her no freedom. She had to get away. But now she was soaked and the horse would get pneumonia again ...

She went on, too miserable to think properly. She came to the high hedge and stared at it. The hoofmarks ended here. Blaze had gone over it; had gone over *that*? He must be lying dead on the other side. Where did it go, anyway? She was off her own territory, six miles away from her home by road, though only four miles away across the cliffs. She followed the hedge and came to a gate and pushed it open.

She knocked on the cottage door. A huge black cat came to the window and looked at her, but nobody answered.

She walked across the yard and a dog barked, suddenly, making her jump. She whirled to face him as he came towards her.

Jack Savage came out of the stable, and Debbie saw Blaze. She ran past the old man, put her arms around the horse's neck and was rewarded immediately by the big dropped tongue. She was shivering so much that her teeth chattered. Jack Savage was about to tell her what he thought of her when he saw how wet she was, and when she turned towards him he was horrified by the expression in her eyes. She had endured enough misery. He changed his mind.

'Your horse will be all right,' he said. 'You'd better come into the house and get warm yourself. You're in as bad a way as he is.'

Debbie couldn't speak. She followed him, and as she walked into the living-room, the heat hit her, and she collapsed, dropping neatly and swiftly to the floor.

Jack Savage stared at her, wishing Mrs Pemberthy were there; but she only came on Tuesdays and Fridays and today was Saturday. She was visiting her married daughter in Exeter for the weekend. He lifted the girl and laid her on the settee. Tremors racked her; he was afraid of the dangers of exposure; she had endured appalling weather; and he did not know what to do. He had never had a daughter; only sons and grandsons. People would talk if he kept her there. Yet he couldn't turn her out.

There was only one thing to do.

He phoned for an ambulance and the men promised to be there within twenty minutes. He was not very far from the town. He banked up the fire, and turned on a heater, and wrapped a big bath towel round Debbie, who had lapsed into unconsciousness. He had no idea who she was.

He was thankful when the ambulance came and the men undressed her and dried her and wrapped her in his enormous pyjamas and more blankets and took her away. They promised to tell the police about her and the horse. He would visit her in hospital. Meanwhile, he had better get back to the horse. He worked on it until he was sure it was as dry as he could get it and then packed straw over its back and put a blanket over the straw, knowing that that way air would get to the coat and any traces of dampness would dry off under the rough stalks, instead of soaking into the rug.

He made a warm mash and watched the horse feed. He shut the stable door and went inside, to drink a stiff whisky before starting to cook his evening meal. He was hungry and he was very tired indeed.

He ate, his mind only half on the food, scarcely knowing what it was he had cooked. He could still see that incredible leap over the hedge at the bottom of the garden. The horse had landed fair and square; no sign of damage to his legs. Luckily the ground was well dug there. But he might have slipped and killed himself.

It was late, and the old man went out to the stable and checked both horses. Colonel had recovered from his fright and was tugging at his haynet. The strange horse was standing, thoughtful, and offered Jack Savage his tongue in greeting. A nice-mannered horse; a well-cared-for horse. He had been wrong in his first impression. Jack wondered who the child could be. He went indoors, intending to phone the vet, but he was out of breath, and his head ached, and he'd have to rest first. He stretched out on the bed and fell asleep. It was nearly one in the morning when he woke. He couldn't ring the vet now. The hospital would have contacted the police about the girl. Jack began to wonder if he had two waifs on his hands. He lay awake, the past suddenly vivid in his mind; and knew, without any doubt at all, that he wasn't cured of horses; that he was aching for horse talk; for a horse to school again; for the thrill and fun of entering for the races; the excitement of winning; the measuring of one horse against another; planning a career for the new young entry; dreaming of might-be's in the future; talking over the great horses of the past.

He could not sleep. He went downstairs again and the dog followed him with a deep sigh, having curled himself comfortably by the old man's bed.

Private Jones stayed where he was, on the blanket on the wicker chair, not choosing to disturb his nightly routine.

Jack Savage looked at the whisky bottle, but he never allowed himself more than one drink a day; he wasn't going to get into bad habits, or turn into an ageing drunk with only the bottle for comfort. He made himself a milk drink instead and took out his press cuttings book from the bureau drawer.

This horse had a look about him of Golden Miller. Long ago and far away, but making his presence felt after generations; the horse must have come from the same stock.

And there had been those other horses.

Jack Savage turned the pages, wistfully, longing to be back again where he belonged.

'Molten Gold, trained by Jack Savage, was the winner of seven races in his early racing career, and of over £29,000 for his lucky owner.'

'Will Jack Savage's entry, Rippling River, stand a chance in this year's Grand National?'

He remembered that horse so well; gaiety and courage, but not enough stamina to take it round the gruelling Aintree course. Its jockey had pulled it up, thinking the race too hard and Jack Savage had known he was right; somehow, Rippling River had never fulfilled his early promise.

And Jack Savage had never had a winner in the Grand National. It was the only victory that had eluded him. He thought of the horse that had leaped into his garden; a horse that could jump like that, at the end of his tether ... what couldn't he do with a horse like that? He sat on, dreaming of the cheering crowds, and the wild exultation that he no longer shared.

He went wearily up the stairs, knowing himself for an old fool dreaming a fool's dreams; doing all the things he had vowed he never would, longing to go back and relive former glories, to take a horse and train it and show he wasn't past it after all. It wasn't as if he were really old. He was seventy-three and octogenarians had trained before now. Elspeth's death had provoked him into giving up when he should have gone on . . .

He looked out of the window. The moon was a thin band, a half hoop, a broken eternity ring, lying on its back. A symbol of his loss. Stars were bright in the sky. Beyond him, in the stable, he heard the rustle of straw. Two horses, one of them come from the storm, an omen.

Jack Savage picked up the morning paper, and turned to the horoscopes. It was his secret piece of foolishness; he had always consulted the stars before embarking on any project, even though he knew the horoscopes were most likely made up by a committee of cynical men anxious only to fill up space in the paper.

He was Gemini, born in May, born under a dual sign. Quicksilver fast in thought, though now he felt as if his brain were beyond thought.

'Today is a lucky day for you. A newcomer will bring you pleasure and you will start a new career, or gain fame in renewing a forgotten skill.'

It was an omen. He went to bed and to sleep, unaware that the future did hold surprises for him; unaware of Debbie, still unconscious in her hospital bed; unaware of Sam, sitting in Michael Pope's kitchen while Michael and Nancy tried to reassure him and tried to think where Debbie might have gone, with the horse, in the storm. Flowers were flattened again by the hail; one of the greenhouses had been blown down; the unpaid bills were still lying on the dresser and ruin was only a breath away, but Sam could not think of that now.

All he could think of was Debbie. And he wished with all his heart that he could put the clock back; that things were different; that he had been gentle with the child.

'She's only a little girl, Sam,' Nancy had said that night. He had been treating her like an adult; had been making her work for him; had given her no freedom; had imposed his stepfather's God on her; a cruel God, dictating to all of them. He was being punished for his stupidity. His head ached and he wished life were simpler and that he knew what to believe.

He sat, staring into the full cup of tea that had long ago gone cold; he did not see it. He only saw Debbie as he had seen her standing the day before, in the yard in Nancy's clothes, slender, delicate, her cap of gold hair blowing in the wind, while the horse beside her stood proudly, aware of his own strength and majesty.

They were somewhere out there, in the bitter cold night, and he would never see either of them again.

Michal Pope poured himself and Nancy a whisky and put another in front of Sam.

'Drink it,' he said, 'and then you had better sleep in the spare room. There's nothing we can do now. The police will be out looking for her as soon as it's light. They've promised to send a dog and handler from headquarters.'

Sam thought of the miles of cliffs; of the cracks and gullies, and of a horse lying dead with a child dead beneath him. To hell with his religion and his beliefs. They were betraying him. He drank the whisky. Nancy was nursing one of the kittens, holding on to it as if it were a link with reality; terrified that her interference had brought Debbie to this; had made the child dissatisfied with her home, so that she had run away. If she hadn't given her the clothes; if she hadn't encouraged her to visit and see a different way of life . . .

'It's easy to be wise by hindsight,' Michael Pope said, when they went to bed. 'Debbie was going to come out of her shell without you, some time. Sam couldn't keep her in an ivory tower for ever. She saw the girls at school; she was already on the point of rebellion.'

Nancy said nothing. She felt responsible and she felt guilty and she felt sick. She lay awake for a long time, watching the moon cross the sky, listening to an owl, eerily haunting; trying to think of the things she needed to do next day and not to think of Debbie, heaven knew where, perhaps not even alive.

The door had been left ajar. She was very glad when the Siamese brought her kittens to curl up comfortably on

Nancy's bed. Their presence was solace. A tiny furry head cradled itself against her neck and she slept, but she dreamed of a speeding horse with Debbie on his back, swimming off into the sea from which he had come, so short a time ago.

She woke, obscurely comforted, knowing it was the horse that had caused the change in Debbie; the horse that had started the train of events, and aware that if they found Debbie alive, the events were only just beginning. There was no way of stopping the future; or of keeping the clock still.

She dozed again, only half hearing the voices in the other room, where a police handler and a police dog were taking Debbie's scent from the gloves she had left in Sam's Land-Rover.

Chapter Nine

The ambulance men contacted the police, who realised that the unconscious girl was Sam's missing child. There was no sign of Sam when the local constable went to the nursery. The place was locked up, and deserted. Only Mop was there, curled forlornly in the straw. The empty stable told its own story. Tom looked all round, and finally wrote a note which he placed in the letter box.

Sam must be out, hunting for Debbie.

Mop had tried to follow the horse on his wild canter, although the dog was terrified of thunder. When the horse vanished, galloping too fast for Mop to keep up, the little dog fled home and hid himself in the back of the stable, quaking with fear, while the devils in the sky hurled their light at him, and howled with rage.

Sam could not sleep.

He left the Popes, intending to go home, but he turned instead on to the cliffs. He took his torch and began to search, trying to remember Debbie's favourite walks, scanning ditches and gullies and small hollows, lest she had been thrown from her horse, and Blaze had bolted and left her lying there injured.

He clambered down the steps and walked at the edge of the tide, afraid the sea might have claimed both his horse and his daughter.

There was no sign of either of them, anywhere. They could have travelled a long way. Surely Debbie hadn't set out to ride to her grandmother's home? If only he had thought more about the child. If only . . . they were the bleakest words in the world.

Somewhere in the darkness an owl called, its haunting cry echoing Sam's own misery. The sea was a remorseless monster, beating against the shore. A half moon flung deceptive shadows. The cliffs plunged sheer into the water, which surged under the stars. The wind seared his cheek. It was very cold. On another night his thoughts would have been with his crops and the money he might be losing. Tonight he could think only of Debbie; not so long recovered from rheumatic fever, out, God knew where, saturated by the storm.

Worry flared to such a point that he could not think. There was a dark bulk under the cliff. Was it Debbie, with the horse on top of her? He ran, and an angry seal woke and lumbered towards the sea, her calf beside her.

He tripped and fell, and the light of his torch went out.

He was helpless.

He would have to go home, walking cautiously, afraid he might slip and injure himself, and then he would be in trouble. No one knew where he was. He began a nightmare scramble through the dark, grabbing for handholds, sliding on wet seaweed, once putting his leg, calf deep, into an unseen pool.

The softly-surging sea was calling for him.

Debbie. Debbie. Debbie.

He climbed the uneven steps, stopping halfway to sit, chilled and exhausted, wondering what to do next. There was nowhere to go. The house would be deserted and empty. He went instead to the greenhouse, to make coffee and warm himself, gaining a little comfort from the scent of flowers that filled the air. He sat down in the armchair beside his office desk and fell asleep.

Had he gone indoors he would have seen the note, but it did not occur to him to do so. He woke, stiff and stupid, to find Mop waiting in the yard, to see that it was only five o'clock and still dark, and to take another torch and blunder out, hoping the dog might lead him to Debbie.

It would have been sensible to phone the police; it would have been sensible to stay at home, but he was beyond sense. He could not think properly; he could not sit idly; it did not occur to him the police might have been trying to contact him. Later, he wondered why; now, there was only the moment and the driving need to find Debbie, the certainty that she and the horse had come to grief and nobody could help him.

'Find Blaze,' he said.

It was an old game. Usually Blaze was somewhere in the fields and the dog ran to him. This time Mop set out for the place where he had last seen the horse. Across the grass to the top of the cliffs, to the tiny hollow where Debbie had slept, and there Sam found the hoofmarks.

Deep, indented, the imprints of a panicking horse. Terror seized Sam. Suppose the horse had bolted over the edge of the cliffs? He ran, following the trail, developing a stitch in his side and a pain in his chest. Surely the child hadn't been on the horse when he galloped like that? Yet there was no sign of her, anywhere. He hunted on either side of the track; every bush, every thicket, every hollow.

He came to the hedge.

The hoofmarks ended.

There was no sign of damage to the thorny bushes that grew so thickly. The horse had gone up and over. How in hell could he jump that? And what of Debbie?

Sam followed the hedge to the gate and saw Jack Savage, neatly dressed in breeches and jacket, already working on the horses. Jack couldn't sleep either, not with such a beauty come into his stable; he hadn't seen a horse like that in years. He stared at Sam as he came into the yard; filthy, his wet trousers clinging to his legs, unshaven and red eyed, a wild man, come from nowhere, shaking with exhaustion.

'That's my horse,' Sam said. 'Where's the child?'

Jack Savage stared at him.

'Didn't the police get in touch with you?' he asked, appalled by the thought that the man had obviously been hunting all night for his daughter. 'I asked them to find out who she belonged to; I was sure someone must be looking for her. She's in hospital. She was soaked and exhausted, and it wasn't wise to leave her untreated.'

Jack Savage was so dismayed that he found it hard to put his thoughts into words. He wanted to make amends, feeling guilty, although the fault had not been his. 'Come inside and ring the hospital,' Jack said. 'There's sure to be someone on all night; and they'll want to know about her next of kin.'

He cursed himself for the clumsy words; it sounded too much like death.

He led the way indoors, talking too much to make up for his unease, switching on the electric fire, putting on the kettle, alleviating guilt by over activity.

Sam was already looking up the hospital number, was dialling, was waiting, his fingers tap-tapping impatiently on the polished table, while Jack set the cloth and cooked bacon and eggs, made coffee, put out food for Private Jones and for Major, wishing he had made sure that the father had known about his daughter; somehow, he could have found out; have done more to help, instead of leaving it all to others, who hadn't done their job. It never occurred to him that Sam might have omitted to go to his home, and so missed a message.

Sam's drumming fingers stilled. The hospital had answered at last. But there was more delay as the nurse on the night desk phoned through to the ward, and then told him, impersonally, that Debbie was safe in bed, but was very ill. Exhaustion, exposure and complications caused by her recent bout of rheumatic fever. Sam, edgy and irritable, thought he detected censure in the tone. He could visit at eleven. Debbie was on the danger list. He hung up the receiver and sat staring bleakly, his private nightmare brought to life. He looked at the clock. It had moved four minutes only while he had been talking. He seemed to have been there for an eternity.

And he was afraid.

He accepted Jack's offer of a bath and a shave; tried to eat the breakfast that had been cooked for him; tried to make conversation. Jack ate too, frowning, wishing that life were easier; wondering at the story behind the man and the girl and the horse; wishing he were younger and more capable of coping.

'Try to sleep in my spare room,' Jack suggested. 'Then I'll drive you home to get your transport. I don't run a car; I have a horse and trap.'

So that was who he was. Sam had heard of him; dismissed as an old eccentric by the rest of the village. He rolled wearily on to the bed, and fell asleep almost at once.

He moved in a daze when Jack woke him, but had to rouse himself to drive to the hospital. Jack, left behind at the nursery, looked around him. There was work waiting here and no one to do it. He went off to see Nancy, knowing that she would help anyone, and only too well aware that he himself was in her debt for various kindnesses in the past. He had placed Sam now; the village grapevine kept everyone informed. Sam had the reputation of being a religious fanatic and a cruel man to his daughter. None of it seemed to be right, Jack thought, and wondered briefly what the village said about him.

Sam reached the hospital and was told to wait. He stared out of the window of the waiting-room, at trees and neat lawns and ducks swimming on a lake. He was vaguely aware of others in the room, but all his thoughts were with Debbie.

There was no need for purgatory. He was there, already. His wife had died through his stupidity; he should never have married her and taken her to live so poor a life; now his daughter would die too, through his own neglect. He seared himself with blame. The immaculate girl on the desk looked at him, cold-eyed, and he thought he detected accusation in her attitude. He was raw with anxiety, ready to be hurt by a glance or a misplaced word, desperate for someone to whom he could turn for comfort.

There was nobody.

It was time to go up; in the empty lift; along the corridor, past a ward where children laughed and talked; walking on parquet floors polished to an insane slipperiness, his footsteps frighteningly loud.

And then the tiny ward and Debbie under the oxygen tent, her face remote, her breathing laboured, her eyes closed, her appearance so fragile that she looked as if one sharp movement would blow her away.

He couldn't even speak.

She didn't see him or recognise him. She was trapped in a world of pain, her chest impossibly tight, her breathing labouring as she ran endlessly after a bolting horse that would not stop or answer her commands.

'Blaze, Blaze, Blaze,' her lips said, over and over.

'Who is Blaze?' the nurse asked, fingers on Debbie's pulse, eyes on the second hand of her watch.

'Her horse,' Sam answered, his voice sounding like a rusty saw. It was all he could do to speak.

He sat on the chair beside the bed, longing for Debbie to look at him; to recognise him; to need him. He remembered her as a tiny girl, running and playing, prattling endlessly; and then riding Blaze, excited by the horse's movement; bending over the flower pieces, working beside him, often late into the night.

He was a madman. If Debbie died . . .

The nurse brought him a cup of tea. The doctor came, grave faced and silent, looked at her, and went again.

The clock ticked on.

It was no use asking if she would recover. Nobody could know. The silent room was islanded in misery; only that constant weary little voice went on repeating the one word, over and over. Blaze.

Dear God, Sam said, praying to a kinder God than the one he knew. To Debbie's God. Somewhere in the preceding hours he had come out of insanity and absurdity to recognise his fanaticism for what it was; born of misery and fear, without rational basis. Others were right and he was wrong. If Debbie lived everything would be different, from now on. He needed to appease his God; Debbie's God granted favours, to those who needed them.

He looked at the bed.

Nothing had changed.

'You can rest in the next room,' the nurse said. There was pity in her eyes, but Sam misinterpreted it as blame. 'I'll call you at once if there is any change.'

Sam could not rest. He was reminded of the nights spent at the hospital when his wife was ill. This hospital; perhaps this room. He sat in the armchair by the window watching the world carrying on living, never caring about him. He would never sleep easy again if Debbie died.

He went back to her bedside. She moved restlessly, and again came that whisper.

Blaze.

If only they were back again, last week, last year, fourteen years ago. How different life might have been. Why had he wasted it? He could not think of anything but his own guilt; he was responsible for this. He was being punished for his arrogance.

The nurse returned with a photograph; a Polaroid picture of Blaze. There was a note with it.

'For Debbie; get well soon, Bob.'

'I think you should go home,' the nurse said. 'We'll ring if there is any change. She has pneumonia; drugs work wonders, but they don't work miracles. You still need time. She doesn't know you.'

It was an indictment.

Sam propped the photograph on the bedside table.

He went downstairs and out into the hospital drive. Jack Savage was sitting in the Land-Rover.

Sam stared at him bleakly.

'I thought you could do with company,' Jack said. 'Michael Pope rang the hospital and Bob drove me over. I've nothing to do all day and you need help. Nancy told me there must be orders to fill; I'd be glad of something to do myself. I'm going rusty; nobody uses me and I'm not that old. I don't like being put out to grass.'

'If Debbie dies,' Sam said and couldn't finish the sentence. He let in the clutch, put the Land-Rover into gear and drove out into the town. Only minutes later the high lanes enclosed him, cutting out the sky.

Later Sam remembered little of that week. He bunched flowers, and Jack made up the orders, put them in boxes, labelled them and Bob or Michael took them to the station. Somehow he coped with routine work; ate and washed and shaved and slept and fed the animals; drove daily to the hospital, knowing Debbie was no better. Jack, looking around him, saw the signs of struggle; knew the stories he had heard about Sam were untrue, idle gossip fostered by malice, or by a desire to create a sensation by news of others; and Sam in his turn was dimly aware that Jack did not merit the stories told about him. They were gaining an increasing respect for each other.

Nancy had come to help; she was there, making meals, answering the phone, unobtrusively comforting Sam without his being aware of her compassion, jollying Jack whose loneliness she recognised, worrying too about Debbie, so that each time she answered the phone her muscles tightened, afraid of what she might hear.

And then the message came.

Debbie was worse.

Sam was in the Land-Rover and out of the yard, exceeding the speed limit, caring about nothing. He had to get to the hospital fast. His tyres screamed as he turned the corner.

'Jack,' Nancy said. 'What will Sam do?'

Jack was bunching flowers, working speedily as if there were no tomorrow. He could not answer. Nancy began to write the labels. The busy clock ticked away the destructive minutes, and outside rain soaked the ground, and hissed softly down the window panes.

Debbie had been moved into a side ward. Sam stared at her; the oxygen tent had been taken away and she was breathing more easily, but she was a shadow of a child, looking up at him from eyes so remote that they frightened him.

'I can't make it out,' the doctor said. 'She's given up. She's like a small animal that's made up its mind to die. She ought to be improving; her temperature is down and the drug has had some effect. But she isn't making the slightest effort to co-operate with us; she's lost the will to live.'

'Debbie,' Sam said.

She looked at him, at a point beyond him, and her eyes remained remote. Sam knelt beside the bed, and took her hands in his. There wasn't the slightest response. She did not look at him. He tightened his hold, forcing his will into her, trying to make her listen.

'Debbie. Blaze is all right. He's fine. He'll be able to come home as soon as you are well enough to look after him.'

There was a flicker in the blue eyes. And then nothing.

Sam sat helpless, looking down at his daughter.

'Blaze. They can't sell Blaze. I want Blaze.'

'Debbie!' Sam's grip tightened. He was fighting now for her attention. 'Debbie, you can keep Blaze. Do you understand? You can keep Blaze.'

'I can keep Blaze? Honestly?' It was only a whisper, but she was looking at him now, her hands moving slightly within his own.

'Honestly. I promise; whatever happens, Blaze is yours. I'll see to that. You can ride him and jump him; he's safe now, and well looked after and will come home as soon as you do. Now get well, quick.'

'Blaze.' Debbie whispered. Her hand tightened over her father's hand. A moment later her eyes closed.

Sam looked up at the doctor, terrified.

'She'll be OK now,' he said. 'She's fallen asleep. It's the best thing that could have happened. She'll be tons better when she wakes; and now she knows she can keep her horse . . . ' he smiled. 'Funny creatures, girls. My own daughter's horse crazy too. There's something about the relationship of a girl and a horse that seems to satisfy a deep need in some children. Come back first thing tomorrow. She'll be awake and asking for you by then.'

Sam wondered if Debbie would ever ask for him again.

Jack Savage was writing out the last label when Sam arrived home. There were flowers for the Market as well as special orders from shops that bought direct from Sam. Sam checked them.

'Thanks,' he said wearily. 'And that's not adequate . . . you've no idea what a help you've been.'

Jack Savage poured boiling water on to the coffee powder he had put in two cups.

'I've enjoyed it,' he said truthfully. 'I've lived near the village for two years and still feel a stranger. It takes a long time to accept a newcomer. I led a very busy life; I trained race-horses; there was always something going on. Now I'm stuck out here with nothing to do for most of the day; only one horse and my dog, and the old cat. It's soul-destroying. But I couldn't keep on the business; it wasn't fair to my son.

No fun inheriting when you are so old it no longer matters. For all that, I wish to God I had started up again. I'm pretty fit and I've an active brain and I'm just rotting away.'

The telephone rang.

'Nancy asked us over for a meal; I'd completely forgotten,' Sam said. 'She says Bob has gone over to see to Blaze and your hunter. And nothing to worry about. Bob's pretty efficient with horses. He helped a lot with Blaze.'

'I'll be glad to eat. I haven't been so hungry in years,' Jack Savage said as he followed Sam out to the Land-Rover. Mop watched them go; Major had been lying at his master's feet all day. Now he climbed carefully into the Land-Rover and flopped down, his head leaning on the tailboard. Mop, suddenly jealous, jumped up too.

'That dog's missing the horse,' Sam said, as he drove through the gate.

'He'd better come home with me; it will help the horse settle if he's been used to having the dog around,' Jack said.

Nancy had been busy; she produced sausages and apple sauce and masses of fluffy potatoes; peas that she had grown herself in the walled raised gardens that Bob and Michael had built for her, so that she could weed the beds from her chair. She grew enough vegetables to pack her freezer every year.

She had made a sherry trifle, and little rock buns; and girdle scones, which she served with raspberry jam made from her own raspberries and with cream from the Jersey cow down the road. Cleo had been a patient of Michael's and her milk and cream now came daily by way of gratitude.

Sam was relaxed for the first time for days, enjoying the warmth of the big shabby room, enjoying the kitten that curled on his knee; thinking of Debbie, soon to come home; and knowing that he had a great deal of planning to do. Things would be different, now.

'We've a proposition to make,' Nancy said, as Michael poured brandy for himself and Jack Savage, and she added cream to Sam's coffee. 'Please think about it carefully, Sam. You could help both of us, far more than you realise.'

'Me help you?' Sam stared at her. 'I'll do anything I can, but . . .'

'We'd like to come into partnership with you,' Jack said. He never believed in beating about the bush. Straight out, and no messing. Tell the truth and shame the devil. He was not a devious man.

'Look,' Nancy said. 'Jack's bored to death and needs occupying; and people seem to think my brain has gone along with my legs. I'm often treated like a mental cripple. I don't think of myself as a cripple. OK, I'm stuck in this idiot chair and can't walk, but it doesn't stop me doing anything I want to do, except dance and climb mountains and ride a horse, but I've learned to live with that. I need a job, Sam . . . I could learn to make the posies and nosegays and bouquets and take that off Debbie's shoulders; I can write labels and bunch flowers and fill boxes; I can keep accounts; I can make phone calls and take phone calls; there's a load of things I could do, and enjoy doing, and I don't want paying; if we make a profit, then I get a share and if we don't make a profit, then I've had fun and occupation and felt useful again. Sam, you've no idea how much time I have during the day; OK, I fill it, somehow, but a lot of things I do are time-fillers; done because there isn't anything else to do, to stop me from feeling sorry for myself.'

'And that's my problem, too,' Jack Savage said. 'Rattling around alone here; I hate it. My wife was my business manager; I haven't much head for figures, so I gave up when she died; but I do have money to use. It's wasting away just now. Where the hell do you put money these days? In a falling market? I lost hundreds of pounds that way two years ago and got out; there's not much return in the bank or in building societies; but your place could make a fortune with the money behind it. Scrap the fields and build more greenhouses; go for heated places and be independent of weather; you could grow tomatoes and grapes; and prices go up all the time. We could do very well, the three of us. But there is one provision.'

Sam was sitting bemused, staring at them.

'Yes?' he said.

'That horse is a jumper; he's brilliant. He came over that hedge of mine like a winner; and if he can do that when he isn't halfway fit, he can win the Grand National and to spare. I've never had a National winner. Let me train the horse; let Debbie learn to jump on him. We can put her in the local show-jumping competitions and she can hunt him, qualify and put him in point-to-point. In about two years' time he'll be perfect for Aintree; one of my son's jockeys can ride him. And we can use his winnings in the business. Sam, I'd give my soul to train that horse; to get back into the swim again; to have a share of the action; to plan his races; his daily routine; to get him fit, up to peak, and keep him there and win that race. It's the only race that no horse I've trained has ever won. I had a horse come fifth once. That's the nearest I've got, though I've had winners in almost every race in the calendar. I've a horse to beat all comers there in that loose box of mine. And he's Debbie's. Nancy told me how she found him. She did a great job on him. We even have a name for him when he runs. Sea Mystery.'

Nancy laughed.

'M.Y.S.T.E.R.Y? or M.I.S.T.E.R.Y?' she asked.

'Maybe just Sea Mist,' Jack said.

'Or Sea Mister,' Bob said. 'Horses have very silly names.' He had just come into the room and was busy spreading jam and cream on the remaining scones. 'He's a gorgeous horse, Mr Trelawny. Gentle as a lamb. So's your hunter,' Bob added, awed by Jack's white hair. Nancy smiled to herself. Bob was rarely impressed by anyone older than himself. He tended to be very casual.

Sam was drinking his coffee in a dream; the thought of money to help him; of people working with him, was heady. But he had to be fair.

'Look,' he said. 'I'm in debt; badly in debt. It will take at least five hundred pounds to clear my debts and there will be more. Greenhouses are expensive; oil costs a fortune and the price rises all the time. The bottom could drop out of the flower market too; people are hard up and have no money to waste on luxuries. Luxuries go first.'

'Then we use our wits,' Jack Savage said decisively. 'I've a comfortable income from my son, far more than I need. I'm a director of our business; working on his scale there is still money in horses. He's doing extremely well. I have no need of the money from my investments. It's more of a nuisance; I pay a fortune in surtax. I sometimes feel I'd rather throw it all away than pay out as I do. I started from nothing and earned every penny and now it's treated as if I have no right to it at all. I don't see any fun in that. I don't need to provide for my sons or their families; they're all doing very well. I don't give a damn if the whole lot goes down the drain. It's insane to sit on a fortune. It's not enormous – but it would go a long way to help. Put the money to use; and maybe one day we can sell out when we are all sick of it, and share the proceeds between us to repay me for what I put in. But let's get at it. Clear those debts, and put up more greenhouses and let us come and help and free that girl of yours for some fun; she's only a baby still. Four more years and she will have to learn to knuckle down to life; but not yet.'

'Can I think it over?' Sam asked. 'I'd like it; very much; but let me get the figures straight and show you the facts. I feel it would be cheating you otherwise.'

'We can make a go of it,' Nancy said. 'I worked it out for myself; with three of us working and no wages to pay, we can make a profit weekly anyway. I worked out what you earned with the flowers I've helped with; and we can cut the overheads in a lot of ways. I suspect we can cut the telephone bill for a start as I can write letters and organise clients; we can advertise. And we can aim some of our produce at the summer visitors. For instance if you plant strawberries in the lower field, we can invite them to come and pick their own; and potatoes might do well this year, with shortages everywhere. You can get the facts about those and put in a plan to plant some and see what happens; and I've always had a yen to grow orchids. I've got a tiny orchid house here; Michael had it made specially for me, so I can get my wheelchair inside. With a good big greenhouse with wide alleys I could play about with those; and the local shops could sell pot plants; Michael can deliver on his rounds; he's all over the place. It's not a vastly busy practice, Sam, it would be fun; you'd be a benefactor. Please, let us come in with you.'

'You've no choice,' Michael Pope said, fitting himself into his sheepskin jacket. 'They'll nag you till you agree; so why not give in gracefully? I think they're right. Jack will be over daily to be with the business so it will be easy for Debbie to get the jumping lessons she needs; and Bob would help with that, in his vacations. He won't be here much, but he comes and helps me with the practice for his holidays, instead of going somewhere else; he has to do that anyway; so he will be down for a good part of the year.'

'If you're sure,' Sam said. It all sounded too good to be true. He would wake up, and find he had been dreaming. It was absurd.

'I'll just ring up and find out how Debbie is before you go,' Nancy said, wheeling herself over to the telephone. The smallest kitten jumped to her shoulder and purred loudly as she lifted the receiver.

'Get down, Nut,' she said, and he slid into her lap, still purring.

'She's taken some soup, and is sleeping again,' Nancy said. 'They say she's comfortable, which means she's on the mend. Yesterday when I rang up they said she was still on the danger list. Go home and sleep, Sam. We'll be over to-morrow to take on whatever there is to do, and you can go and see Debbie.'

Sam dropped Jack Savage at his home, and watched Mop leap out of the Land-Rover and run over to the stable, and whimper to Blaze. The horse answered eagerly, his neigh of welcome startling Jack's hunter into neighing too. Major clambered down from the back, and walked regally towards the house, his plumed tail waving, his long-eared golden head held proudly. Only then did Sam realise the retriever was holding Jack's gloves in his mouth. Private Jones appeared from the stable door and purred loudly, and then saw Mop and hissed. Mop leapt sideways, and then, as Jack Savage laughed and opened the stable door, the dog ran inside and lifted his nose to the horse. Blaze bent down and touched the dog with his muzzle.

'You can't separate them,' Jack Savage said. 'Funny how often a friendship strikes up between animals of different sorts. Private Jones is devoted to my horse, and often sleeps on his back so long as he's rugged. Colonel doesn't like the claws in his hide. He shakes the cat off; I suspect the affection is somewhat one-sided and the cat is after warmth rather than company.'

Sam drove back through the moonlit lanes. He parked the

Land-Rover, and walked out on to the cliffs. The sea was a faint glitter in the sky. A slim moon hung over the steps to the beach. Waves creamed softly against the rocks. Sam stood in the field, looking out, feeling peace creep over him for the first time in years.

He remembered a couple of lines from a poem learned long ago.

> The grey sea and the long black land;
> the yellow half-moon, large and low . . .

He probably had it wrong, but it described the scene before him perfectly and for the first time for years he stood, looking out, enjoying time to stare, and time to think, and time to listen to the soft sound of the waves.

He felt as if he were at the bottom of a long road that wound up a steep cliff; there were miles to go before he reached the top; but there was now a faint hope on the horizon and perhaps the prospect of reaching a goal instead of drifting from day to day, knowing that tomorrow would bring even worse problems.

An owl called; a cloud hid the moon. Sam went indoors. Nini was waiting to be fed. He was very glad when at last he could crawl into his bed.

Chapter Ten

Jack Savage, visiting Debbie in hospital, knew that plans were important; having hope; and a future; a goal to look forward to. And he knew, as he handled Blaze, that the horse had character; had potential, and was the sort of animal on which he too could build dreams. He told Debbie something of his own past life; of the horses that had raced and won; horses that had brought him luck; horses that had been quiet, gentle creatures in their stables, allowing pigeons to roost on the manger, yet going out full of courage to fight every inch of a race, and win at the end, by sheer persistence and will power.

They began to make plans for Blaze. Debbie would learn to jump; she would learn dressage; Jack would teach her all he knew; and Blaze would jump his way through the local gymkhanas; would hunt, would race in point to points, would win and go on to novice chases, would fight his way up until he won the Cheltenham Gold Cup; until he won the Grand National. He could jump like a hero and he had recovered so well from his ordeal in the storm that there was no doubt about his stamina.

Debbie was eager to go home and start working with the horse.

'You've both got a lot of freewheeling to do,' Jack said. 'Get fit; you've all summer ahead. Walk with your horse and swim; it's time you had a rest. You won't need to help your dad so much now Nancy and I are partners.'

The frost had proved a good omen, instead of a killer; Sam's greenhouse flowers fetched high prices. When Nancy began to pick and box her orchids, she found a ready market. There were very few orchid growers. Jack promptly designed a greenhouse for her, where she could work between the staging from her wheelchair, with sliding doors that she could operate without need of assistance from any-one. He knew exactly how much Nancy valued being independent.

By the time Debbie came home summer had started and the orchid greenhouse was half completed. The fields had been cleared, and planted with potatoes; the stable had been rebuilt. Jack and Sam and Bob and Michael Pope had worked together on it. It was draughtproof and strong, with a good concrete floor that was easy to clean, and a feed store beside it to make it more convenient for Debbie. Jack had brought over a saddle that he'd been reluctant to sell, as it had belonged to his wife. Debbie fondled the gleaming leather. Her old saddle was falling apart.

There were hooks for girths and reins and bridles; there was even a box for Mop, which Jack had made in his spare time, enjoying working with wood. He had always loved making oddments for his stables; but there had been no incentive to make anything up to now at his new home.

'We're going to feed you up,' Nancy said, as Debbie began to get about again. 'And you can show me how to make the lovely headpieces you did for the Mevagissey wedding. Several people have asked for similar tiaras for their bridesmaids but we've had to say no.'

Life was suddenly excitement. There were always people about. Jack had two grandsons. He had never had a daughter or a granddaughter, and Debbie and he soon became firm friends. He had wondered if he would have difficulty teaching her to ride, but she had gentle hands and was surprisingly capable of firmness. Blaze found himself mastered, and began to work for Debbie. Before, they had only played.

Debbie and Sam had an absorbing new interest, as both of them were captivated by the horse. Sam was becoming hooked, and often exercised him, enjoying the relaxation, recapturing a long-ago thrill. Blaze became the main topic of conversation; his care; his treatment; his diet; his future. Jack was a constant companion, and life began to take on a new dimension. Even Nancy caught the bug, and began to study racing form, trying to work out what kind of future their acquisition might have.

Within two years, it was hard to remember that Sam and Jack and Nancy had not always been partners; that Nancy had not always been there for Debbie to talk to; or that Bob had not been part of the family. As soon as he came home for his vacations he rode over to the farmhouse, and he and Debbie plunged at once into plans. Debbie only rode in the local events when Bob was home. Half the fun was gone if she had to go alone.

By the time Debbie was seventeen she was jumping with confidence and had a number of rosettes to prove it. Sam had given her one of his discarded ties, and she pinned her trophies on this, hanging them beside the picture Bob had taken of Blaze, which she had fastened inside the feed-room door.

She looked at the rosettes every time she went to make the horse's meals. Four fourths; five thirds; fifteen seconds; and three firsts. There were also two cups and a rose-bowl and a small shield on which was a horse's head. Jack had bought a horse box and a Land-Rover.

One of his ex-jockeys had become stable man, chauffeur

and batman, freeing Jack to help Sam and coach Debbie. Les Pagett was now part of the family too, and took the orders to the station daily. They were a good team, all of their lives now focused on the horse. Their own race-horse.

Jack was brisker, invigorated, excited, leaning on the rails at the events, talking horse talk, discussing riders and techniques, back where he belonged, with an interest he had never dreamed could be his again.

That winter he took Debbie hunting to qualify Blaze for his point-to-point race. It was hard to believe that the horse had never faced crowds. He was confident when he jumped, without any show of nerves. He loved an audience and waited for the gasps that sometimes accompanied a spectacular leap. He had a knack of getting himself out of trouble if he were too close or too far away and Jack had taught Debbie to leave the judging to Blaze. Check him, or urge him, and his stride was wrong and they were faulted.

Debbie enjoyed the Hunts, at first riding at the back, as far away from the action as possible. She had dual feelings about the fox. Foxes killed their chickens, and needed keeping down, but when she thought about killing she felt sorry for the fox. On two occasions when she saw him break away and run free, she kept her mouth shut, feeling guilty, but glad that he had got away.

Jack pored over the racing papers, thinking about the entries; about the distance from home, as Debbie was now working for her school certificate. She did not yet know what she wanted to be. She did know she had to work with animals; she couldn't take an indoor job. That would be total deprivation.

She ran everywhere. Sam, watching her, found it hard to believe in the change in her. She was now nearly as tall as he, tanned from being out of doors every spare moment of the day, her blonde hair cropped short, gleaming against a neat head. Her eyes were always alive with eagerness, as she dashed home from school to be with her horse, and took him out for his evening exercises. Blaze watched for her, calling over the stable door which was now too solid for him to escape; greeting her with his tongue, waiting for her to change and come for him, while Mop, now elderly and a little sedate, trotted out with them and lay at the gate in the field which was fixed up with jumps that Jack and Sam had built for her.

When Bob was home he brought his horses and they practised together, dropping into an easy companionship, teasing and quarrelling and arguing endlessly, both of them only children in need of company. It didn't matter which was home; Bob was in and out of the farmhouse and Debbie always welcome at the vet's where she now often held an animal for Michael or helped with anaesthetics, freeing Nancy for the orchids which were now both a passion and a very lucrative mail order business. She had widened her interests and corresponded with growers all over Britain. Debbie preferred the more usual flowers. The orchids made wonderful centrepieces for flower arrangements and she was so good at these that some of the local organisations asked her to do their decorations for them; for fetes and festivals, and the amateur theatre group; and for Masonic dinners. Debbie was building her own bank account, most of which was spent on Blaze.

Sam had altered too, although he did not realise it. Life was easier, was pleasanter, and he and Jack Savage had become firm friends. Jack was more than grateful; he enjoyed the status of an adopted grandfather, coming over for meals on Sundays, staying for supper, often talking late into the night, unknowingly teaching Sam a great deal about the racing world, which had been totally foreign to him, although his real father had been a jockey before starting the riding stables.

Blaze was the centre of all their lives and all their hopes. Debbie wrote long letters to Bob when he was away, mostly about the horse; Jack planned and worked and dreamed for him; Nancy stopped to admire him, envious of his strength and mobility. She found an unexpected sense of freedom watching him jump. She could imagine herself on his back instead of Debbie; the horse was part of her dreams and her daydreams too.

For Debbie he was all-important. Nothing else mattered so much. All her future was bound up in him. One day she looked in Jack's paper to find out the size of the prize money for the Grand National; if she could win that with her horse, and have half of the money, as her share, she could pay her father back for everything he had spent on Blaze; could contribute towards the family expenses; could feel she was not wasting money at all, but earning it.

She began to read about racing; about the great horses that dominated the past; and to pick Jack's brains. He was as eager to share his knowledge, finding her a most receptive pupil. Together they began to read the race forecasts; the lists of winners; the form of each runner; to make notes and compile a complete dossier of all the horses that were running.

'With that in mind, we ought to be able to pick the right race for Blaze when he starts,' Jack said. 'No use putting him against veterans when he's young and green. He needs to have a bit of competition but not too much; I don't want him to lose heart. He's too good to spoil.'

Debbie thought of the pattern of the last two years; the show-jumping and the hunting; the summer out to grass, resting and growing fast; and then the autumn, and the gradual build-up of work, of getting him fit, of feeding him properly and grooming him properly, of caring for him so that he did her credit.

He was now just over eight years old; maturing, his splendid coat shining, the powerful muscles rippling as he ran. He sometimes galloped over a field belonging to a friend of Jack's who trained his own horses and had a splendid farmhouse and grounds fitted with everything needed for teaching the horses their job. Once Debbie had ridden him in a race against two of the stable horses, feeling for the first time the exciting power as Blaze, at first finding it hard to keep his pace, had suddenly accelerated and passed the other two horses.

'You've a lad with stamina there,' the other trainer had said, as she slid off the horse, laughing. 'Those two of mine are very young and inexperienced, but I thought they were pretty good. Your boy has what it takes. Look after him.'

As if she needed telling.

Riding Blaze was high excitement. Debbie no longer hunted just to qualify him; she hunted for the fun of the gallops; for the chance of riding over land which would normally be forbidden to her; for the new experience it gave her; here along a lane and over a high wall; over a hedge and a ditch; high over a dyke and layered brush-wood fence beyond it; over rough land and over turf; always pitting her wits with those of the horse against the country, yet watching to ensure that neither of them came to grief. Jack would not allow her to ride hell for leather, devil-may-care; she had to think of others; had to be careful never to interfere with the hounds or get in the way of the Hunt officials; had to make sure she never took a big risk that might end in a broken neck for her or the horse.

He taught her as he had taught his sons and had started to teach his grandsons; but he had never had a pupil like this; and he had never had a horse like this. Blaze could hunt all day, and apparently be worn out, yet after a half hour rest he was as fresh as the morning again, and eager for yet more work, if they had been fools enough to give it to him.

Debbie learned to look to her horse first; she might be saturated and covered in mud, and starving as well after a hard day's outing, but the horse had to be dried and rugged and made comfortable before she could change her own clothes and satisfy her appetite. Hunting was ten times more fun when Bob was with them, and occasionally Michael Pope came too, leaving his practice in the hands of a colleague a few miles away. He never took a long holiday, preferring to have odd days off when business was slack.

'She's a great girl,' Les Pagett observed one day, as Debbie went clear to win her first major trophy. The red rosette and the cup were shown to Blaze who was used by now to wearing gay colours on his head, but was much more interested in the pony nuts held in her cupped hand.

By now Debbie and the horse were well known; everyone admired the lively chestnut, who adored being the centre of attention, holding court for the children, regally taking sweets from them, whether they were peppermints or dolly mixtures or liquorice allsorts, occasionally stealing a swift lick at an ice cream negligently held, once taking a loaf of bread from a parked van, before Debbie had realised what he was about to do. She had no money with her and had to go and pay the baker later that day. Fortunately the man thought it funny. After that she took great care to give parked vans a wide berth.

Blaze knew the sound of the hunting horn; as soon as he heard it his body tensed, ready to run; his ears went up and his head went up and he began a little pirouette, a tiny dance step, sideways on, so eager to go that it was hard for Debbie to restrain him.

'He's a grand horse,' the Master said as he signed the last certificate. 'I suppose you don't want to sell?'

Debbie would as soon have sold herself into slavery as sell her horse.

That night they parcelled the certificates to register at Wetherby's. Blaze was qualified; and now where would he run? Everyone was brought into the conference; Sam and Jack and Nancy and Michael. Bob was away from home, but Les Pagett, who had ridden for more than ten years, was an important part of the set-up; outside in the stable Blaze looked over the door, watching them through the lighted window, Mop in his box beside the manger, and Nini sitting on a rafter looking down. Blaze nosed his hay-net, quite unaware that he was the most important creature in the place, and that everyone was dreaming dreams about him, fired by the desire to give him his chance at the biggest jumping race of them all, by now accepting Jack's frequently-repeated dictum . . . 'We've got a future Grand National winner. No mistake.'

Chapter Eleven

Far away in the Midlands others were dreaming dreams. Matt and Sally were at breakfast in the little room that overlooked the stable yard. The lads were busy; horses were being led in from exercise; a mare was being schooled in the nursery field. Another mare was being led out of the yard into the paddock, her foal following gaily at heel.

From here they could watch everything. At the first sign of trouble, Matt would be outside.

'I'm fed up, and I'm damned tired,' Matt said suddenly. 'Nothing's gone right in the last two years. There's no point to anything. We need a break. There's the National coming up and I haven't a thing to enter; nothing of the quality we need. It's like watching food set in front of you when you haven't any teeth.'

He banged his hand down on the table irritably.

'Joe's expecting complications with Binnie's foal. I can't stand listening to the mares when they're in pain. Let's get right away and forget horses.'

Sally was looking at him consideringly, one eyebrow raised. 'What's up with you?' Matt asked.

'You do have one soft spot,' Sally observed. 'It's about the only thing I like about you.'

Matt stared at her.

'Don't go overboard about it, will you?'

There was a sudden squeal from the yard.

'Damn it, that's Mercenary. I told you that new boy of ours was no good. He ought to be in a zoo. Behind the bars in a monkey cage.'

Matt ran from the room, slamming the door behind him. Sally watched as he raced into the yard and then slowed to a sedate walk. He disappeared into the loose box as Joe came into the room.

'He's edgy as a cat with a breached kitten,' Joe said. 'Take him away, Sally. He's upsetting the lads and that upsets the horses and I've enough on my plate. I wish to heaven he could get a horse for Liverpool. Unsatisfied ambition's worse than an itch you can't scratch. And he needs a son.'

Sally stared at him, and Joe flushed fiery red.

'I'm sorry,' he said, but it was too late. Sally had run from the room, and Joe followed, turning into the yard, cursing himself. He was tired and overworked and Matt wasn't helping; he was hindering, fine with the horses, but giving all the staff the rough edge of his tongue. It didn't do; it made for an unhappy establishment and you couldn't run horses well unless everybody pulled together.

No use telling Matt and he shouldn't have said that to Sally. God knew she'd tried and it wasn't her fault.

By the time Matt came in again, Sally was packed.

'What's that for?' he asked, having totally forgotten their earlier conversation.

'You said you wanted to get away. Let's cut and run,' Sally said. 'Right away from here; we both need a break. Joe and the vet can cope with Binnie. They don't need me. Nobody needs me.'

Matt looked at her for a moment, but her head was turned away from him, and he couldn't see her eyes.

'Please, Matt,' Sally said. She had to get away; away from memory and away from failure. She couldn't go on here. Not like this. She had too many rivals, and much as she loved the horses, she was also jealous of the time they took and the attention they needed, so that she was entirely superfluous.

'OK,' Matt said. 'We'll go. I'll brief Joe and we'll leave after lunch. No horses for a week. That suit you?'

It was beginning to snow as they drove off, but neither cared. The chance of a holiday had lifted their spirits, and Sally felt like a girl, free from everything that trapped her. Matt whistled as they drove. He hadn't realised how tired he was. Work went on and on, seven days a week with night alarms as well.

'Champagne every night. The best of food and no worries,' he said.

Sally laughed.

'In England? In March?'

She watched the country. They were driving South, through little villages that looked as if they hadn't changed over the centuries, past woods and fields that were also unchanging so that she could imagine the tramp of the Legions as the Romans came to rule. There were no rabbits and very few birds. A circling buzzard was a startling sight. So was a hare, bounding over the fallow. She put her arm down and fondled Sheikh's ears. The dog was lying at her feet. They could always find a room where the landlord allowed the dog. She would never leave him behind.

He was the only family she had. But she tried to remember he was only a dog. He was never spoiled.

By the end of the fifth day they had drifted down to Cornwall and were staying in a little inn called the Lugger, where the food was first class, and the beer even better.

'You won't find anything horsey here,' Sally said, looking at the prints on the wall, of Dickens' characters, in rich colour, and all their peculiarity; fat Sarah Gamp and slimy Uriah Heep; jovial Pickwick, and Fagin, bearded, bent and sly. They were in a private sitting-room, a wood fire blazing in the chimney, coffee on side tables, relaxing after one of the best meals they had eaten all week.

'You'm needing food, me dears,' the landlady had said, her voice soft and her eyes kind, as they came in, stamping their feet with cold, after a walk on the cliffs with the wind roaring in their ears and the crashing sea a constant echo.

Matt went to phone Joe. He couldn't rest until he knew that all was well.

'Binnie's foaled; a bit difficult, but a nice little filly, and both well. And there's a local horse show and dog show combined tomorrow, in a field nearby. The landlady says it's always fun. I know what we said; but would you like to go? It's only for the kids.'

The kid he'd never teach to ride, Sally thought, but said nothing.

'Let's go,' she said.

'It'll be good for a laugh. Do you remember how we met? You'd jumped your horse the wrong way round the ring, and I'd come off at the lowest jump and there we were, a couple of kids ourselves, comforting one another for being such fools.'

It seemed a very long time ago. Sally went to bed light-heartedly, after an evening spent remembering old times and absurd events; coming off her horse at the water jump at one show, going home soaked, while Matt had gone over another jump and his horse had stayed behind, having refused to go. It had been fun in those days. Where had all the fun gone now?

Next day was cold with a lowering sky and a bite in the air. A king-size breakfast, of bacon and sausage and egg and potato cakes, of scones and jam and cream, put them both in a good mood. Sally dressed in a sheepskin coat and a little bright cap, to cope with the weather, while Matt collected an immense sandwich pack which their landlady had made for them, and had added to it a huge flask of coffee liberally laced with brandy.

'You'm going to be very cold, me dears,' she said, in her soft burr.

The weather deterred no one. The field was already seething with competitors and spectators by the time Matt and Sally arrived. Sheepskin-coated men and women talked together, admiring dogs and horses, talking show talk. Odd snatches drifted past Sally, who suddenly remembered her own show days and was amused.

'The judge was either stoned out of his mind or blind as a bat to give a First to that knock-kneed dog. And it was nervy as hell.'

'Never saw anything like it . . . knocked down every jump, and then sailed out of the ring, over the benches and out of the show. Never stopped for five miles . . .'

Sally relaxed, suddenly catching the atmosphere; the hope and the excitement; the eager competitors with their dogs; the children trotting on their ponies; the makeshift barriers of post and rope; the mud and the puddles and the crowd round each ring. She watched a lovely Alsatian bitch win her class, to a cheer and a shower of handclaps, the dog herself eager and happy, the owner grinning, flourishing the red rosette, shaking hands with those she had beaten; in another ring a small Jack Russell was working an obedience class, unexpectedly proficient. Sally had never thought of the tiny breeds putting up such a show. He wouldn't know his placing till far later that day.

Competitors with set faces were schooling dogs; children put tiny ponies over minuscule practice jumps. One little boy with curly hair and brilliant eyes was walking his pony gently to and fro, steadying him, using all the control of a professional. Sally recognised a child from a home where horses mattered; perhaps were bred; certainly were cared for and ridden. His small importance hurt her; she would have taught a son of hers in the same way.

And then she forgot him as Matt grabbed her arm.

The under-eighteen show-jumping had been going on for some time; Sally had been watching the dogs, as a change from horses, and had not watched the jumping.

A blonde girl on a magnificent chestnut rode into the ring.

'Aren't they beautiful,' a voice said behind them.

Matt was riveted. The horse was splendid and he knew it, every inch of his body proclaiming that he was handsome, was special, and it would pay to watch. Jack had groomed Debbie well; she knew how to make an entrance, her horse dancing his way into the arena, pawing the ground and dipping his head in a little gesture that delighted the crowd. Jack had taught him deliberately. Blaze responded to applause. It excited him as much as the hunting horn.

Debbie was nervous, as she always was. Her breakfast had consisted of two bites of toast, eaten under protest, and three cups of coffee, which she wished she hadn't had. It was the one thing she never could conquer; that first knee-knocking entry into the ring, aware of all eyes on her; many critical; some disapproving; some hating her because she took the trophies from them.

And then there was no time for nerves. They were beginning to circle the field. She knew the layout. She and Jack had walked it twice the day before, after the earlier heats had ended. She knew how to approach each jump; knew the way round, though she was still afraid she might miss a fence or take a wrong turn and find herself faced with an impossibility.

Blaze saw what lay ahead of him and settled at once, knowing his job and loving it. Down the field and up and over with inches to spare, landing clean, and away to meet the next one, a five-barred gate, just right. And then round and over a water jump, down the field to a treble, over it safely, judging it perfectly, swinging round to take a wall, down a stretch that seemed endless, to a double, to finish the first clear round, over a second five-barred gate. They had faced far worse when hunting.

Blaze flashed his tail and pirouetted, knowing he had done well, and Debbie leaned down to pat his neck and stroke his mane, her eyes searching for Jack and Les. Up went their hands, thumbs up, grinning; beside them Nancy was laughing excitedly, and Sam's face was one broad smile. Debbie trotted past them on her way out of the ring.

'Lovely girl,' Les said, and that was high praise.

'What a horse,' Matt said. 'I wonder what his breeding is. He's a thoroughbred all right. What the devil's he doing down here?'

'Funny old story, that horse,' a farmer said beside them. 'He was washed out of the sea. God knows how he got there. No one hereabouts would throw a horse over the cliffs to end his life; and no one had lost one. I always thought he was maybe stolen from somewhere else, got free and bolted off, and went over the cliffs in panic. Nobody knows a thing about him. Young Debbie there rescued him and brought him on, made a proper job of him. And Mr Savage is training him; got hopes of the Grand National in a year or two, they say. He's just done his hunting season and qualified himself for the National Hunt.'

Matt looked at Sally. The same thought had crossed their minds.

'How long ago did he come ashore?'

'About two years ago. Wild, that night was; one of the wickedest nights of the year. Blew half Sam's . . . that's young Debbie's dad . . . greenhouses down. Several ships got wrecked that night; and an oil tanker went aground. Had a lot of trouble with that slick.'

There was a gasp from the crowd as a horse jumped wrong, and the gate went down. The young rider, losing her seat, fell, but picked herself up and mounted again and went on.

'That's the stuff heroes are made of,' the farmer observed, but neither Matt nor Sally were listening. They were looking at Blaze.

'It couldn't be,' Sally said.

'A stormy night; shipwrecks; an oil slick; and a horse swimming ashore. Why not?' Matt asked. 'Is it likely there were two horses in the sea that night?'

'Matt. The *Daisy May* went down nearly fifty miles from here. No horse could swim that distance; if he did how could he survive? He'd be pounded on the rocks. Just think of the shoreline.'

'He's a look of the Miller, that horse. Khazan had a look of the Miller. That's what attracted Joe; you know how he hero-worshipped that horse. He grew up with the Miller's story; went to watch him run every time out and there's never another horse like the one you first give your heart to. Except the great horse you own and train yourself.'

It was hard to watch other horses. Nothing else mattered except the big chestnut.

Matt went over to Debbie. She was joking and talking excitedly, patting the horse on his neck. Matt wanted to look at the animal; wanted to sum up the girl. If it were Khazan he would offer her another horse. He had several potential jumpers in his stables. She would never know the difference between one horse and another.

'That's a fine horse,' he said, stroking the animal. The horse looked at him, a considering stare, recognising a man who understood his kind.

'Isn't he gorgeous,' Debbie said. 'He's the most terrific jumper; he goes over like a cat, up and up, without any telling; there isn't another horse to touch him, anywhere in the world. We're building him up for the National, aren't we, Jack?'

Jack Savage looked at her, wishing she hadn't revealed his plans. But the child was excited; it had been a great round and she was beginning to work as part of the horse, to know the pleasure of partnership.

'They're a team,' Jack Savage said, and Matt's hopes began to fade. This wasn't going to be as easy as he had hoped. Not half as easy. Every movement the girl made told of her knowledge of the horse, of her pleasure in him, of his worth to her; it wasn't just a girl and a horse. And another horse wasn't going to be the same.

He turned his head and saw Sally watching him, and watching the girl. He knew by her expression that she appreciated that this was a special relationship; one of those rare, once-in-a-lifetime things that happened between human and animal.

And he knew too that if this horse were Khazan, he was going to wreck the relationship. It was his horse and he wasn't going to give up *his* dream; he was entitled to realise his passion; he had seen the horse first. He had heard of it; had sent Joe to buy it; had paid for transport, and been balked at the last.

He stood back as Debbie rode off, his hunger apparent in his eyes. It wasn't fair. Life never was. His thoughts seethed.

'You can't do it, Matt,' Sally said.

He could do it and he would do it, if the horse were his,

and he was ninety per cent certain that this was Khazan. There couldn't be two of them; or two horses lost at sea that night.

'She has to learn,' Matt said. 'Life is made up of disappointments; I lived with mine. Now it's her turn. She'll forget. She's young; plenty of time for her dreams to come true. I've one that will never come true; and I'm not going to be done out of this one.'

He could have said nothing crueller.

Sally walked alone back to the Lugger, all pleasure gone. They were all in for heartbreak. How much, not even she realised.

That night in the Lugger, Sally and Matt quarrelled over the horse.

'You've got the insurance. You don't know it's Khazan. You can't wreck that child's life; the horse is the most important thing she has; he's everything to her. You've only got to watch them together.'

'She's growing up, soon she'll have boyfriends; there's probably one already; she'll forget horses. They're only a passing phase in most girls' lives. He won't get the training he needs down here; he's wasted; used for jumping and hunting, with all that potential inside him. And besides, he cost me a packet. I'd like to get my money back on him.' Matt was angry, pacing the room, filling it with too much passion, and Sally was tired. It had been bitterly cold and she had become more and more uneasy, especially when Matt had been talking to Debbie. Sally remembered being seventeen; with her own first good horse that won prizes for her; remembered the years of show-jumping; the bitter disappointment when she failed to make the England team; the enormous pleasure she had from touring the shows; a pleasure that faded with age and responsibility. She had been heartbroken when Little Ballerina developed cancer in the hock, after an injury, and had to be destroyed. They couldn't take the horse away. She prayed that this wasn't Khazan.

'Look. We can settle it once and for all,' Matt said, his voice angry. 'There's no need to go all feminine and soft-centred about it. Drive back and take over at home and send Joe down. He spent two days with the horse. He'll know if it's our horse or not. And Paddy and Dan will like to know it's alive. They were very upset when the *Daisy May* went down.'

There was no use protesting. Sally went to bed unhappy and could not sleep. She left early, driving fast, wishing they had never gone to the show.

Jack Savage, seeing Matt walk to the post office next morning, felt his own worries return. There was nothing for Matt here, except Blaze. And if Jack knew his horsemen, Matt would make an offer for the horse and refuse to take no for an answer. And if Matt were interested, others might be; and anyone could steal the horse from Debbie's stable. Mop wasn't much of a guard.

That night Joe was startled to see Sally arrive home alone.

'Matt's found a horse that he thinks is Khazan,' she said. 'I'm to take over and you're to drive down and look at him. It came ashore after that gale. A girl has looked after him all this time.'

'It can't be Khazan, he'd have had to swim miles,' Joe said.

'Joe,' Sally said. 'Do you have to say it's Khazan? Matt got the insurance money . . . that child adores the horse.'

'The horse is alive, so no one's entitled to the insurance money,' Joe said. 'And if it's Khazan, it's Khazan. What's meant is meant . . . and for a reason. God knows what reason, but there is a reason for everything. Can't get away from that. And it's a miracle in itself if the horse is still alive.'

Sally went indoors. She couldn't settle and went out to look at her mares. They greeted her, each one in her own way. Sally stayed in the stables for a very long time, checking every horse, petting every horse, noting that water buckets were filled and that everything was shipshape. The house was too large and too empty.

But she had to go indoors at last. She sat with Sheikh at her feet, dozing and twitching as he dreamed of chasing rabbits. All she could see was Debbie's excited face and the eager way the horse had greeted her, and the proudly-held rosette.

She was pretty sure that this was Khazan. And Matt would never change his mind; he had set his heart on the horse two years ago, a horse to win the greatest race of them all for him; a horse to appease a ruling passion; a horse that would enchant the crowds, that would hit the headlines, that would bring the stable fame, that would make Matt a name to be remembered in the only history book that mattered to him.

She would have loved to have the horse two years before, but now all she could think of was the gap his going would cause in so many lives.

Not even Sally realised how many people were now involved with the horse, pinning their hopes and dreams on him, planning for his future, planning to win the most exciting race in the world with him, dreaming dreams and feeding on hope.

Even Sam now felt the horse was a good luck symbol. His business had flourished with the horse.

Jack and Les had been down to the Lugger; had been talking to Matt in the bar, though no one had mentioned Khazan. Now, at home, they sat on either side of the kitchen table, while Major slept on the hearthrug and Private Jones stretched out on the bench by the window, which was next to a radiator.

Neither of them spoke. Both of them had now heard of Matt's ruling passion, to win with a great horse; and if the horse was taken from them both men would be left desolate, with no future to plan for.

'Suppose he offers Sam a fortune,' Les said.

Jack said nothing. The thought in his head was far worse than that. Sam could refuse a fortune; but that horse had come from somewhere; everyone had forgotten by now that it wasn't really Debbie's. Finding's keepings wasn't really a view that would be taken by the law.

Both men lay awake that night; so did Matt, driven by a wild excitement, by the conviction that this was the horse he had lost that had been miraculously restored to him, and when they took it home, all their fortunes would change.

And about time too.

Blaze stood in his stable, safely hidden from the night. Mop snored in his basket and Nini was curled in the straw. Everything was well with his world.

Joe drove swiftly, not allowing his thoughts to wander.

Motorways needed total concentration and he was not used to the Jaguar. It was like riding a thoroughbred after years on a twenty-five-year-old mare. He stopped briefly to eat, and then he did think of the horse. He had longed for a really good race-horse before he retired, and that wouldn't be so long now. He was over sixty; well over sixty, though not even Matt realised that Joe was nearly as old as Jack Savage. A man couldn't go on forever, but he needed to fulfil that dream. He thought of Red Rum's owner, over eighty before he had got his Grand National winner, having cherished the thought all of his life.

Joe didn't want to wait that long. If this were Khazan . . . if he had swum all that distance then his staying power was fantastic; he had more than what it took to run the gruelling Aintree course; to go on and on and up and over every obstacle, pounding over turf, never faltering, with that last grain of effort that would take him past the winning post. Joe had adored the horse, even in that short time. Excitement built in him at the thought that Khazan might still be alive.

Joe finished the foul coffee, made a face as he ate the tasteless sweet, and went back to the car. Out on the motorway he concentrated again, clocking up the miles, coming nearer and nearer to his goal. He arrived late in the afternoon. Matt was too impatient to allow him even a cup of tea. He got straight into the car, took the wheel and drove over to Sam's.

Debbie had come from school and was just saddling Blaze. It would soon be too dark to see. The horse was dancing for her, impatient to be worked; eager, excited, his tail swishing. Debbie laughed and gave him a playful slap on the neck.

'Stop it, you great booby. How can I saddle you when you won't stand still?'

Matt watched as the horse looked at her, an impish gleam in his eyes, sucked in air and swelled out his belly. Debbie, trying to tighten the girth, gave a sigh of exasperation.

'Very funny. And now can you behave and let's have this thing tight. I'll be off if you don't give up playing the fool.'

The horse glanced at her. She knew she had to use her

voice on him, and said, 'Stop being an idiot. We're going to work.'

The horse stood still.

Matt glanced at Joe. This was no besotted owner spoiling a horse; Debbie had been well taught by Jack to stand no nonsense. A little bit of jollying, and then she was firm. The saddle on, she swung up, not noticing the men at the gate.

Across the yard and neatly over the fence without bothering to open the gate. It was plainly a familiar routine.

Debbie settled, walking the horse at first; exercising him gently; trotting him round the field, and then she began to practise dressage. Blaze loved learning; and it was a good performance.

'He's been taken into capable hands,' Joe said.

Matt was watching, eyes eating the horse. Every muscle rippled as he walked; the gleam on his coat did credit to his feeding and grooming; the set of his head showed his pride in himself; the gently-swishing tail showed his spirit. Debbie turned towards the jumps, and then was away; up and over, and on, not a foot wrong, never making a mistake, knowing each other so well that both she and the horse could have gone over them blindfold.

Jack Savage and Sam came out of the greenhouses to watch. Jack saw Matt and Joe and his mouth tightened.

'That's a grand horse,' Joe said, his eyes on the horse, now certain that this was the horse he had bought in Ireland; the horse he had thought lost at sea.

Debbie trotted over to the gate.

Joe reached up a hand and Blaze dipped his nose to the hand, delicately. Joe could see the ideas ticking over and waited breathlessly. The tongue was suddenly delivered straight into his palm, and he squeezed it.

'He knows you,' Debbie said, and then saw Jack's expression and her own changed to dismay.

'I bought him in Ireland, two years ago,' Joe said. 'I'm positive it's our horse. The ship went down at sea. I thought he had drowned.'

'I found him on the beach,' Debbie said. Her voice was remote, coming from a long way away, reluctant to be heard. Her throat was tightening and she held on to Blaze, afraid she would fall. Even Matt noticed her white face and realised this was not going to be as easy as he had hoped.

'Debbie saved his life,' Jack Savage said. 'The horse was exhausted; was cut about from the rocks, and developed pneumonia. She slept in the stable; never left him for a moment. It was a miracle that he lived at all; without Debbie, he would have died.'

'We never dreamed that he could have survived,' Matt said.

'We'll buy him from you,' Sam said. They couldn't part with the horse; not now, when everything was going so well for them; when Debbie was beginning to win on him; when they all, even Sam, had set their hopes on the Grand National for him in about three years' time, realising his potential. Debbie was going to stop show-jumping with him and Jack intended to bring the horse on for racing; for real racing. They all had plans.

'Have you got £15,000?' Matt asked. Joe just stopped himself from gasping at the highly inflated price. 'The insurance money has to be paid back; the horse is alive; we claimed on false pretences. I took the money for him, thinking he was dead. Now I'll have to refund it.'

Two years ago Jack had had the money, but now he was heavily invested in Sam's business. They were beginning to make profits, but not that kind of profit. His son might lend him the capital for the horse, but he would be asking Martin for a risky loan; the horse might never make the grade. It wouldn't be fair. He could break his neck in his first race.

They had no choice. Jack knew that from the moment Matt set eyes on the horse; there never had been any choice.

'Can you prove this is the horse you lost at sea?' Jack asked.

'I'll get his breeder or his head lad over,' Matt said. 'Will you take that as proof? And the sale documents and the horse's pedigree? His name's Khazan; he was well known in Ireland before we even bought him.'

'We've no choice,' Sam said.

'I'll compensate you for the time and trouble; you've done a magnificent job,' Matt said.

'Nothing can compensate us,' Debbie said, and then could not face them any more. She led Blaze away, and took him to the stable, where she unsaddled him and groomed and fed him and bedded him down for the night, trying to pretend that this was like any other day; that nothing had happened to change her life, and feeling as if the horse were under sentence of death. She might just as well have let him die. She would rather he did die than think of him in someone else's hands; perhaps not well treated; being forced to work, to race, to win, with an eye all the time on the possible money-making potential and none at all on him.

Jack came into the stable, and looked at her. Debbie turned her back.

'It's going to be hell, Debbie,' the old man said. 'The end of your hopes and mine; I know that. But there is one consolation. Mr Keene and Mr Garnery are good people; they have a reputation for kindness and run their stables well. Blaze will get first-class care; Mrs Keene is a darling; everyone thinks highly of her.'

'We don't know that he is their horse,' Debbie said. 'Let's wait till the Irish people come over. They could be wrong. They didn't own him for long.'

'We have to face facts,' Jack Savage said. 'No use kidding ourselves. It's one of those things. Life has lots of them in store for everyone, Debbie. The horse won't live forever, either.'

'I could take death,' Debbie said, and squeezed the big tongue that was suddenly offered to her. She turned and ran out of the stable, and Jack finished bedding the horse, and fixed the haynet. Nini was stretched on the rafters. The little cat jumped down and curled neatly on the rug, and the big horse turned his head thoughtfully to look at the cat.

Nini purred.

Mop was already in his box. He never left Blaze once the horse was bedded and fed and left for the night. Jack stood looking at the trio, his eyes worried. He was old and inured to disappointment. There had been so many, all his life. He remembered the Cheltenham Gold Cup; he couldn't remember the year but he had had the most beautiful grey entered; Silver Swansdown. And the horse had made a small mistake halfway round the field; a tiny mistake, but he had landed on mud and slipped and broken his leg. There was nothing to be done but shoot him. It was the kind of break that never would heal. Jack had watched the race. His horse had been far ahead of the rest of the field. He had congratulated the winner with a very tight throat.

There had been his own little pet mare, Sisanna, who died producing her first foal; and over the years there had been too many disasters; better not to remember. There had been triumphs too. Three weeks after losing Silver Swansdown he had won three races in a row at one meeting with three of his untried babies; one of them went on to create racing history, winning and winning and winning again, and that had been his own horse, so that the prize money was his; and no need to know it had belonged to an owner, who merely paid the bills and never did the work.

Sam was standing by the door.

'It's tough,' he said. 'I'd been lulled into thinking no one would ever claim him.'

'We'll get over it,' Jack said. 'Debbie's going to be the problem; that horse is her first love; at seventeen you haven't got the stamina or the experience to meet total loss. She'd have coped if the horse had died; but she will hear of him; he'll be running for someone else. I feel like getting drunk tonight.'

Sam looked up at him in dismay. He had changed a great many of his views in the past three years but he was still firmly teetotal.

'I don't mean it,' Jack said. 'Though Les will go on a bender if we lose the horse; I don't think there will be any doubt about the recognition.'

'There's still a chance.' Sam knew he was being foolish, pretending a child's make-believe of living happily ever after. Life wasn't like that.

Paddy flew over two days later, and Joe drove him down to Cornwall. There was no doubt about the horse. Forlornly, Sam and Debbie and Jack and Les and Nancy looked at photographs, and Debbie looked hopefully to see if there wasn't something about Blaze that would prove he wasn't Khazan.

There was no doubt whatever when the horse saw Paddy, for he greeted him in delight, neighing when he heard his voice, giving the man his tongue over and over again, butting against him and searching pockets that quite plainly had always contained special titbits. There was a special titbit now. Paddy had a doughnut in his pocket. Blaze ate it, ecstatic.

'I bet you never discovered that,' Paddy said.

Debbie shook her head, too miserable to speak. Paddy looked at her, and looked at Joe, and knew that life had too many hidden punches.

'I'm sorry,' Paddy said. 'It is Khazan. I wish it wasn't . . . you've done a great job. But Mr Keene did pay a fortune for him; the highest price we ever got for a horse.'

There was no choice.

Blaze had to go.

Debbie couldn't bear to wait.

'You can take him now,' she said, and walked away from them all to sit on the beach staring blindly out to sea. Once she had run away with the horse; now she had grown up and knew that was no solution. Some time later Bob came, saying nothing, but sitting close, his hand in hers. He had heard about Matt's recognition of the horse from Nancy, when she phoned, and had immediately hitch-hiked down, to be with Debbie, though he knew there was little he could do. Except be there.

That night Debbie hurried past the empty stable, and went to help with the flowers. Matt had organised a horse box, fast. There was nothing else to do. No horse to train and ride; no horse to care for; no tongue to greet her; no wise-eyed head watching for titbits, hopeful always that she had something exciting hidden in her pocket. She glanced out of the window. Nini was sitting on the wall; Mop was lying by the gate, watching the road down which the horse box had driven their companion away. They knew the box always came back.

That night everyone picked flowers as if their lives depended on it. The bunches were made and the boxes stacked and driven to the station. And there was nothing to do but go to bed.

Debbie went first and sat in the moonlight, listening to the silence. No rustle in the straw. Then came an eerie howling. Mop was crying, in the empty stable. She ran down the stairs and brought him in. He sat on the window seat all night, staring out into the darkness, refusing to be comforted.

Sam too lay awake, wishing he knew how to help Debbie. But she had to learn and no one could do that for her.

Les sat in the kitchen, drinking steadily, far into the night, while Jack Savage sat in his little study, with Major at his feet, staring into the fire, wondering how on earth they would fill their leisure. He had thought he was hardened to disappointment.

Now he knew that somehow, you never did get used to it. Each time was harder than the last.

Chapter Twelve

Everyone congregated in the yard to see Khazan arrive. He was a miracle horse, come back from the dead; all the lads knew about him. One of them, being enterprising, and not averse to a quickly-earned fiver, had told the local press. The item, read by a racing reporter for one of the big dailies, made a headline story the next day. Photographers filled the yard.

The horse that returned from the dead.

Khazan was already beginning to make his own history.

He had his own ideas about that. Ron, the heavy-handed boy, was given the horse as one of his two. Matt still managed to keep a number of lads in the stable, and tried to give each horse as much attention as possible. But no matter how he tried, Khazan was never going to get the attention he had had as Blaze, in a quiet stable in a yard near the sea.

Khazan could not see out. He was used to watching everything that went on. He was not fed at his usual times, Ron forgot his water and gave him water straight from the tap, a crime that Debbie had never committed in her life; his water always stood, to take the chill off it and bring it to room temperature. Also his diet had been slightly changed and he had a pain; not a bad pain, but a little needling pain, a pain that came and went again, and then came back again, making him more and more irritable. He was lonely; he missed Mop and Nini. And Ron, when Khazan, needing to be petted, had offered him his tongue, had said, 'Give over, you great loon,' and shied away from it. Nobody had ever refused to squeeze it before.

Khazan stamped in the straw.

Nobody came. He wanted Debbie. He wanted fussing. He wanted exercise. He wanted to see what was going on. He didn't appreciate the roomy gloom, or the door that was higher than his head; or the pigeons that suddenly flew in, having been used to roosting in the stable when its previous occupant was there.

Normally quiet, he decided to play up. He kicked out, striking the partition with both hind hooves, making a noise so thunderous that it startled him. He bucked and kicked again, and his hoof caught the bucket which flew over with an almighty clang that terrified him further. The handle caught his shin, hurting him.

He squealed and went berserk.

Ron was young and unused to horses; he had only worked with the stables for five weeks. He had his own pony, gentle and old, and wanted to be a jockey. Now, he wasn't so sure. He ran at the commotion and stared at the horse, kicking wildly, his hind hooves thundering again and again against the partition wall. Each echoing thump upset him even more.

Joe raced down the yard.

'What in hell's going on?'

'He's gone mad,' Ron said. 'He's a horrible horse. I'm not going in there.'

Somebody had to go in there. Joe stood at the door, trying to soothe Khazan with his voice but the horse was beyond soothing. The pain in his middle was worse, a knife pain, a wild stabbing, that caused him suddenly to fling himself over and roll, his hooves flailing in the air.

'Bloody hell, he's got colic,' Joe said. 'Go and ask Mrs Keene to ring the vet and do it quickly.'

He had to get into the stable, had to avoid the wildly-kicking hooves, had to get the horse on his feet, had to soothe him and gentle him before he hurt himself badly. Ron had left the bucket in the stall, and that was a dented mass of metal. There was also a pitchfork, which should not have been there either; the lad was impossible and would have to go; he didn't obey any of the rules. If the horse's leg caught the pitchfork . . . Joe managed to grab the fork and tip it through the stable door, and then to put a halter to Khazan, who had paused, exhausted.

'It's all right, fellow,' Joe said softly, but it wasn't all right, for the pain came again, and pain of a type he had never known before, dominating everything, associated with this strange new place and these strange new people who had somehow managed to give him this new and horrible sensation.

He turned his head and bit Joe on the shoulder, just as Matt came in through the door.

'What's got into him?' Matt asked. 'Are you all right?'

'Bruised,' Joe said ruefully. The horse appeared to have recognised his sin. He was standing still, uneasy, every now and again turning his head to look at the bits of him that hurt.

'Colic,' Matt said.

'And homesick,' Joe said. 'That lad of his is no good. Upset him and left the bucket and the pitchfork in the stall; and I'll bet gave him a drink straight from the tap. I can't think of any other reason for this.'

Blaze kicked out again as Ron came running across the yard.

'Walk,' Matt said furiously. 'You know the horse is upset. No need to make it worse. Did you ask my wife to ring the vet?'

'He's coming,' Ron said sullenly. He was a small shock-haired boy. Matt had not liked him at his interview and had been in two minds about employing him, but had been asked to take him on as a favour to an owner. It would be the last time he did that instead of backing his own judgement. There was a lump forming on the horse's shin, and he was again pawing restlessly and unhappily, his mind on his own inside, almost unaware of the people around him.

'I'm not doing that horrible horse,' Ron said, as Matt

closed the stable door behind him, leaving Joe to gentle the animal.

'You're not doing any of my horses,' Matt said, too furious to be polite. 'You can get your cards and go. I've had enough of you.'

He turned on his heel and walked towards the house. Now they would be short-staffed and he didn't know where to get a good lad. So few of them were used to horses.

It was Sally who came up with a possible suggestion.

That afternoon Matt took off for Cornwall again. The vet had been to see Khazan; the horse had been treated, but he was uneasy, restless and plainly unhappy. He showed no sign of relaxing with any of them, and unless they found someone the chestnut could trust, they were in for a lot of trouble. Khazan had been a family pet for far too long. He had never known the routine of a really busy place, where he was left to his own devices inside the stable for hours at a time.

Matt was given his old room at the Lugger. He was suddenly uncertain of himself; he would not be welcome. He had taken away much more than a horse from them; he realised that now. Sally had been talking, and Sally, when she was roused, made some pungent comments. Matt had a horse to offer to Jack Savage; a good horse; one of Sally's own, that also needed extra care and had not settled happily into the stable routine. Sally wanted to race her, next year, but Missmeralda was temperamental; was a shy feeder needing coaxing to eat; and needing far more time spent on her than anyone had available. Yet she had potential. She was a small grey mare, a flyer, though with a mind of her own. She didn't like crowds, or tapes, or starting gates, but given someone's full attention, she might make the grade. Sally had suggested that Jack should train her for them. He and Les between them might have the magic touch required to bring her on.

Jack listened when Matt spoke.

'We don't want charity,' Jack said stiffly. They were sitting in his little study, Major watching them thought-fully, aware of the tension in the air. The dog's head turned towards first one speaker and then the other, as if acting as referee.

'I'm not offering you charity,' Matt said angrily. 'The mare's a bloody nuisance, but she's also very fast and if anyone can give her time she has what it takes; we don't have time. You know what it's like. Sally has our mares in foal; the breeding side's her business. A full-time job. The race-horses are my business; she owns this one. I bought it for her birthday, and it's been a very chancy buy. She won one race, but she's always needed extra care. She's a problem. I know your reputation; you had one or two awkward brutes in your time but you managed them; and you have the time and I don't and I'm prepared to pay as much as my owners pay me; it's a business deal; and I owe all of you for what you did for Khazan.'

'It's what you're doing to us now that worries me,' Jack said. 'Debbie won't eat and isn't sleeping; I doubt if she's working at school either. Luckily Easter's on us and she will get a break; but God knows what she'll do for three weeks without her horse; she spent most of her time with him, or on him, or doing him.'

'I haven't a lad who'll touch him,' Matt said. 'He's playing up. I gave him to one of my new lads, as I thought he was gentle.'

'He's like a lamb,' Jack Savage said. 'No vice in him.'

'He's smashed a bucket and kicked down a partition and bitten Joe,' Matt said. 'He's edgy and unhappy; had a dose of colic, and I'm at my wits' end as either Sally or Joe or I have to do him. I put one of my top lads on his back and he stayed there for exactly five seconds, as the horse decided he was a rodeo bronco and wouldn't allow anyone up.'

'He's always been fussy,' Jack said. 'I suppose we spoiled him. But it didn't matter here. He's a stickler for routine and hates change. What are you going to do about him?'

Jack waited, hoping against hope that Matt would send the horse back to Cornwall to train. Matt wouldn't do that. This was his once-in-a-lifetime horse; he had an instinct, a hunch, that was almost a certainty. This horse would make a winner and go on winning, and he could do with extra money; times were rough and prices high and rising every week. Hay cost a small fortune; everything was stacked against him. No one else would have the credit for his horse.

'I'd like to see Debbie,' Matt said. 'I think she could help me. She knows the horse.'

'She's due any minute,' Sam said, and even as he spoke Debbie came down the lane, walking slowly. There was nothing to come home for. She wasn't yet used to the bleak evenings, without her horse to ride and groom and feed. The hours stretched endlessly and pointlessly. Bob was away, and there were only the flowers; and that wasn't much fun. Mop was lying by the gate. His tail wagged, but he was waiting for the horse box to return. Debbie was no longer important to him.

'Debbie,' Matt said.

She looked up at him, her eyes hostile. This was all his fault and she didn't feel reasonable about it.

'Debbie, please, listen,' Matt said. 'It's very important.'

She watched him, unnerving him by the total blankness of her eyes.

'Look, Debbie,' Matt said, desperately anxious to gain his own way. 'I'm sorry. I can't say more than that: But I need you. Khazan's playing up. He won't let anyone touch him or ride him; he's behaving like a wild horse. He doesn't trust us, and he started off with colic, which unnerved him completely. If you come and help settle him in, it will be granting me an immense favour. I know it's a lot to ask . . .'

His voice trailed away. Debbie was staring at him, her face still totally expressionless. He didn't know what to make of her. He didn't know how to handle her. He wasn't used to girls. If she'd been one of his lads . . .

But she wasn't.

He needed her at that moment more than he had ever needed anyone before. He wasn't a man to ask favours. But the horse was worth a fortune, if he could settle the horse to work, and behave. And Debbie was the only key. No use asking for anyone from Ireland, as Paddy couldn't come and Dan couldn't come and the lad they had now had never known Khazan.

Debbie's thoughts were racing. She wanted to go and be with the horse. She would like to work with horses. She didn't want to stay in Cornwall for ever; but she had never before seen a real chance of getting away without upsetting

Sam. And that she wouldn't do. Perhaps she could stay and work in the stables; perhaps she need never leave Blaze again. She'd never remember to call him Khazan.

'Can I talk to my dad and tell you later?' Debbie said at last.

'I'll come back in an hour,' Matt said, suddenly furious at being in the hands of a girl who was little more than a child; he wanted to shake her. He had thought she would leap at the chance. Now she stood there, as Sally had stood at home saying quietly that she would never agree to adopting a child. Women, he thought furiously, and turned on his heel.

He walked out over the cliffs, descending the steps to the beach, and the crashing fury of the boiling waves echoed his surging thoughts. He flung stones against the cliff, watching them smash and break. He found a level stretch of sand left by the outgoing tide and paced it, to and fro, to and fro, while up above Debbie sat, talking to Jack and Sam and Nancy.

'It's up to you,' Sam said at last. He had long ago relaxed his warder-like attitude to his daughter. Nancy had persuaded him that Debbie had to grow up; had to make her own mistakes and her own decisions. He couldn't shield her for all of her life. Just being alive was a risk. He had done all he could now and it was up to Debbie herself.

Debbie knew that it would be harder next time to leave the horse. She had lost him, she thought for ever. Now he was to be hers again, just for a little while. She had to teach him to trust others; to help him accept new surroundings, when all the time she wanted to bring him home and keep him. She remembered how she had run away.

But she had been a little girl then. Now she was old. She felt very old.

'It will mean everything in the world to Mr Keene,' Jack said gently. He knew, only too well how she felt. He felt the same way himself. There had been something about the horse . . . People who had never lived with a horse might think it idiotic; they could never understand how an animal could become a passion, could dominate your life and thoughts and hopes, could make himself part of you, so that this loss was a major loss, even though you knew it to be absurd.

Being absurd was only being human. Those who didn't care weren't worth knowing.

'I'll go,' Debbie said. She had been thinking of Khazan alone in a strange place, hating every minute; missing her. She had to go. She couldn't let him go through life with the reputation of being a spoiled pet, or a rogue. She had to give him his chance. She knew now, from talking to Jack, just what that chance meant to Matt; just what it would have meant to her. If he did win the National, it would be partly her doing. She had found him and healed him and made him fit, and taught him some of the things he now knew. Some of the credit would be hers, even if the horse were in other hands.

She went outside and watched Matt stride up the path.

'I'll come,' she said, and as she said it, he suddenly realised just what this was going to cost her, and guilt needled him.

'Thank you, Debbie,' he said, meaning it most sincerely and finding the words inadequate. 'Can you come as soon as school ends? Sally will come for you. She'll love having you; she's very lonely as I'm so busy.'

He startled himself again. He had never been a perceptive man. But he knew Debbie shared his passion for the horse. And he had a sudden glimpse of his wife, standing forlorn, looking through the window, watching life go by, filling in her time with things that perhaps were never very important.

He was a thoughtful man as he drove home that night.

Debbie was thoughtful too. She had to pack; and she was taking Mop. Matt had thought the presence of the dog would help the horse. She knew that if she took him he would have to stay behind. He had scarcely eaten since Khazan went away, and was daily growing thinner. Nini was fickle and only asked for warmth by the fire now she hadn't the horse to sleep on.

'Nancy, how will you manage?' Debbie asked. She was always in and out of Nancy's home, shopping and fetching and carrying.

'You're only away for two weeks,' Nancy said, laughing.

'I'll survive. I managed before I knew you. You're spoiling me. Be good for me to stand on my own feet; or at least, on my own wheels.'

Debbie grinned and hugged her. Sam watching, suddenly realised that Nancy mothered them all, even though she couldn't race around. There was always talk and laughter and the room which she worked in was the centre of the house.

'I'll never remember to call him Khazan,' Debbie said.

'Most horses have pet names,' Jack said. 'You can't call a horse April the Seventh or Number Nineteen. They usually end up as Bob or Rotter or Soppy.'

'Make some coffee, Deb,' Sam said, 'and then come and put your wits to work. I can't do my sums tonight. I get the wrong total, or a different one every time.'

'I'll make coffee,' Les said, appearing like a genie from the yard. 'Bob's on the phone and wants to talk to Debbie. We won't be seeing her again tonight. Once those two start yakking it goes on for ever.'

Debbie grinned and ran.

'I'm glad I'm not paying the bill,' Sam commented. Bob's phone calls were becoming more frequent.

That night Debbie lay awake, thinking of the weeks ahead, and Sam watched the moon pass across the sky, and wondered what lay ahead for them all. Signposts to the future did not always point in a guessable direction. He sincerely hoped that Debbie would come home again. He would miss her.

He couldn't keep her forever.

He had to learn, all over again, how to live alone.

Now was as good a time as any to begin.

Sally had a knack of turning a simple journey into an adventure. The Jaguar sped along the motorway, the daunting traffic becoming a source of fun. Even Debbie realised that Sally was a superb driver, and once she had relaxed she began to enjoy the speed. Tonight she would see Blaze again; tonight would be the beginning of a new life, a life in a world very far removed from the quiet Cornish farm. The girls in her class at school had been acid with envy.

They arrived in the dark. The horses were bedded for

the night. Debbie ate sandwiches and drank milk; she hated coffee. She went to bed in a bright room with modern furniture, where the striped curtains matched the bedspread and blended with the walls and toned with the luxurious carpet. She had never imagined such a house. She lay awake listening to the noises of the night. Owl call; a horse neighing; the rustle of straw. Mop was in his box beside her bed. He was bewildered and came to her twice in the night for comfort, poking a cold nose into her neck.

She had never imagined anything like the big yard; the white-painted fences; the smooth fields, more like lawns, and the horses. She watched the mares being led out, the foals following, elegant graceful little beasts, with unbelievably slender legs and dancing steps, breaking into excited gallops as they reached the fields, kicking up their heels, their half formed tails twitching busily when they sucked.

There was bustle everywhere as the lads came to do their own horses, joking and pushing one another, casting sly glances at her. She went over to the stable where Joe had told her Blaze was waiting for his day to begin. Mop was beside her, walking very close, worried by the new sights and smells, trusting no one.

The stable door was bolted. It was also padlocked. Debbie waited while Joe undid the lock. Inside, Blaze stirred restlessly, preparing himself for battle with people he neither liked nor trusted. As Debbie swung the door open, he bucked.

'You stupid nut,' she said, and the horse stood, staring at her. He came to her and nosed her and pushed her and his long tongue came swiftly out into her waiting hand. Debbie squeezed, and pushed him back.

'Silly ass. Did you miss me? Come on, then. Let's make you comfortable. This won't do.'

Her voice was familiar, was reassurance, was a sign that all was well again even if he were in strange surroundings. Mop was sitting in the straw, his mouth open, his tongue hanging, his tail threatening to come off. Blaze lowered his head to the dog and Mop went mad, running round the yard, trying to catch his own tail, ecstatic to find his horse again. Blaze watched him while Debbie began the familiar tasks that she had done for him so long.

Joe watched her, unobtrusive, wondering how she would settle. He saw her fetch water in the bucket and stand it in the sun; he saw the quick competence as she raked out soiled bedding, moving the horse gently, with only a word. He had not realised that Blaze responded to command. 'Over then, let me by.' 'That way, good boy.' 'I'm going behind you.' Debbie chattered all the time she worked.

She murmured softly, almost under her breath, in the old horseman's whisper, never realising that she had picked this up from Les and Jack; a gentle soothing, a soft sssing, reminding Joe of his own grandfather shoeing a horse, keeping up the whistle under his breath.

A big bay gelding in the next stall looked over at her, and Debbie turned and blew into his nostrils, standing still, waiting for a reaction. The horse huffed back, and Debbie patted his neck and laughed up at him.

'No need to be jealous,' she said. 'I expect your turn's coming soon.'

There was feed to mix and grooming to be done, and there was the familiar movement of Debbie's hands against Khazan's sensitive skin; gentle, just right, giving him comfort and confidence. Later, when she saddled him, Matt watched from the window, saw her swing up on his back, and then the walk around the exercise area. No work for the moment. Just settling in, for both horse and girl. Sally stood beside him, watching.

The horse in a lifetime; the one good horse, the great horse they'd all been longing for. Living with Matt and Sally, Debbie began to understand the driving need Matt had to have a horse that could win the Grand National. He had dreamed of it since he was a small boy. Some wanted to be Prime Minister; some to climb Everest; some to write the best books ever; some to dance and some to sing. There were men and women everywhere with ruling ambitions and this was Matt's. And since she knew that Blaze was special, a horse in a million, a future king, she could not blame him. She caught Matt's passion. But Blaze was still her horse. And he knew it.

Blaze had to run and win. He could do it. He was clever. Very clever.

Matt had asked one of the leading jockeys to come and ride this horse and give an opinion.

'I hope we don't have trouble,' he said, remembering Blaze's fury when he was first mounted by a stranger.

'He'll be OK as long as I'm there,' Debbie said. 'And Mop, of course.'

She soothed the horse and held him for Steve Shako to mount. Steve was young and long and lean with dark untidy hair and a sardonic eye. He winked at Debbie as he jumped into the saddle and then they were off, over the turf, the horse flowing along. Blaze settled to work. Debbie was there at the rails, and Mop was beside her, and the horse was at ease and unafraid. The mild colic had cleared up quickly, and now that he was back in a familiar routine he was as fit as he had ever been, and would be fitter.

Round the field and over the jumps and through the gate on a long gallop on hard turf. And suddenly Blaze was away, speeding down the wind, tail streaming behind him, faster than Debbie had realised he could go. She looked up at Matt, but he had forgotten everything around him, his eyes were fixed firmly on the horse, a yearning expression in them, as if he could make time fly by and achieve his ambition tomorrow.

Steve came back to them, dismounted and patted the smooth neck.

'He's quite a horse,' he said. 'I'd like to ride him, if you've no other plans.'

Matt nodded, as if an unspoken question had been answered. It was time to make plans for next season; to work out races; to think about the future. Debbie watched them walk off, and was unexpectedly jealous about being excluded from the conference; Blaze was her horse. She led him back and rubbed him down and rugged him. He was full of himself, jaunty, giving her his tongue, butting against her, pushing her against the wall, rubbing against her shoulder.

'You're a pest,' Debbie said. 'Stand still for goodness sake.'
He stood still, very briefly, and then was off again, keep-

ing up a dancing restless movement that made him extremely difficult to groom.

From that day, time flew. Steve came down daily to ride the horse and get used to him. He preferred not to meet a horse for the first time in a race; he liked to be part of the training and to know his mount. Soon he developed an affection for this one, so that he wanted to be with the horse. Blaze had a magnetic attraction for everyone who encountered him.

Steve was also attracted to Debbie, although Debbie never realised the fact. Her mind, when not full of Blaze, was full of Bob. She wrote him long letters and he answered them briefly, immersed in his own job.

One day they took Blaze to the nearby race-course, when, after racing had ended, Debbie rode Blaze and Matt rode Merry and Sally rode a horse named Tomaselda. Matching them against one another to give them the feel of the course and of other horses around them. It was exciting to gallop beside the rails, to pretend she was a jockey on a top horse in a big race, and that money was at stake. Real money. Blaze forged ahead, remembering racing in Ireland, remembering the old excitement of running against other horses, eager to beat his stablemates.

For all that, Debbie was hard put to it to outdo the others. She reined Blaze, as they reached the winning post, only first by a nose.

'Not at all bad,' Matt said. Joe had been watching, his eyes on the three of them.

'Pretty good, I'd say,' he answered.

Debbie had been elated. Now her mood changed. She was to go home on Saturday. Blaze had settled now. He accepted Steve and accepted his new lad, a good lad who knew horses. Debbie wished she could stay with him; could work in the stables; could be part of the place, rejoicing in his wins, leading him at the races, waiting for him at the winning post.

But she had another year at school. Sam wanted her to stay until eighteen; to try and take her A level examinations; to qualify herself for some career. He didn't feel there was any future as a groom in a racing stable, and

Nancy had persuaded her to consider her future. Perhaps she could be a vet, like Bob.

She went out to say good-bye to Khazan on that last morning. It was as bad as it had been before; worse. He was coming to them for the summer, but he was no longer hers; a horse to be stabled for someone else; a horse she couldn't ride in a show, or continue to train; she wasn't even sure she wanted him to come back to her so briefly. Life was going to be made up of greetings and partings. But there would be next year to look forward to, and the chestnut head watching for her again. She would live from one year to the next, wishing the time between away.

Sally was driving her home.

Debbie could not speak. She had patted the horse for the last time for some weeks; he would soon be back, but she had to leave him now. She had left Mop with him for company and wouldn't even have her dog when she got home.

'Suppose Khazan never wins a single race?' she asked Sally suddenly as they came within sight of the village church.

Sally could not prevaricate.

'Matt will have to sell him; we couldn't afford to keep him,' she said, knowing that to Debbie it would be worse than facing a future in which she owned a part-time horse, and knowing too that there was no merit in hiding the truth.

She didn't want Debbie to go home, but she hadn't told the girl that. It had livened up the house to have Debbie around; it had been fun to go shopping together, indulging in feminine talk instead of stable talk, admiring pretty things. Sally had wanted to buy clothes for Debbie, but had restrained. It wouldn't be fair to Sam.

That night, Debbie lay awake, longing for her horse, while Sally drove home, dreading the silent house, wishing she had a daughter of her own.

Chapter Thirteen

Sam became resigned to racing papers on the kitchen table, to Debbie and Jack talking over Khazan's chances. He was a horse that had already become part of racing legend; his swim, his rescue, his career in Debbie's hands, were all repeated in the racing news whenever the horse was mentioned. His prospects were considered, his future was a matter for speculation. It was fuel for the commentators, who could build him up when they spoke.

Debbie missed him more than she believed possible. She rode Bob's hunter while he was away, but it wasn't the same. Dillon was a steady horse, a gentle horse, a kind horse, but he lacked Khazan's flare and verve and character. Khazan was a horse in a million. Dillon was one of the millions; but not a special horse. Riding him never provided the thrill and exhilaration she had known on Khazan. She was teaching herself to remember his real name. They called him Zan in that stables. Sally wrote often, long newsy letters about the horse, knowing how Debbie felt.

Through her letters Debbie learned their plans.

Khazan came home for his summering. The excitement of having him back was tempered with the knowledge that it was only a brief respite; that all too soon he would be gone again. Meanwhile he raced in the field and rolled; came to Debbie, asking for his doughnut; walked with her down the high lanes, riotous with summer; walked the cliffs to Jack's, where Jack and Les looked at him, noting how he had matured. He was in splendid health.

There was another season, and the horse had gone again, and Debbie was worried about her exams, and Bob was away, and life had no flavour at all. Work and school and more work. A head crammed with facts, and the only relaxation to ride Dillon over to Jack and talk racing talk; or to help Sam with the flowers and discuss her future. She still didn't know what she wanted to do. She would have liked to go back to Matt and Sally, and work with the horses, but Nancy and Jack discouraged her, feeling there was no future there. Bob would soon have finished college and was to become his father's partner. Michael Pope was finding the practice heavy going on his own and there was never a chance of a holiday; locums were expensive.

Racing began and Sally wrote or phoned Debbie to tell when Khazan was running. This was his great season; his build-up to the Grand National with Matt riding him. First he was to run at Cheltenham in the Gold Cup race, with Steve on board. Matt thought he had every chance of winning. He was shaping well. Sally sent his racing dates; some were to be televised and everyone could watch him. There was excitement and there was anxiety. Suppose he never made it, after all? Suppose Matt sold him as a no-good horse?

It couldn't happen.

Khazan's first race was in the North. A race not to be televised. Sally rang as soon as it was over.

'He came fourth, which wasn't at all bad for first time out,' she said.

Debbie had hoped he would run in a cloud of glory, flying in front of the others, first by several lengths. She swallowed her disappointment. Sally and Matt seemed pleased, and though it didn't sound a good result to her, Jack Savage was delighted.

'He was up against real competition in that race,' he said. 'Not a little race for unknown horses; Matt pitched him in head first. I wouldn't have done it; Matt takes risks. He did splendidly.'

It was frustrating to watch her horse on television; never to touch him, never to be able to go up after a race and pat him and give him his doughnut.

Sally did that.

Sally had also fallen in love with Cornwall. She drove down whenever she could steal a few days, finding Matt even more engrossed in Khazan, finding the house too big and even more empty since Debbie had left; with no mares to foal till next year she felt lost. She wished she had hundreds of mares; she wished she had a child to occupy her time; she wished that Matt would remember her sometimes, and not rush out to see that all was well with the horses, so involved in the work and the running horses that she might not exist.

She had never imagined she could be so lonely. She had not even realised that she was lonely until Debbie came to stay and they had time to laugh together and to ride together, and were company for one another in the evenings.

There was always a bed at Nancy's, and Jack loved Sally's visits. She brought him news of the horses; made him feel in touch again, and when she suggested that he provide livery for some of their owners, he jumped at the opportunity. There were always horses waiting; recovering from gruelling races, or needing care and attention for an injured leg, or horses retired, that Sally refused to sell, feeling they had worked well and earned their rest. Matt despaired at times, saying that Sally's soft heart would bankrupt him.

Debbie found herself part of the world of horses again, with two occupants in her own stables, neither of which Sally would race or sell. It made up, just a little, for the loss of Khazan.

She felt the old hunger for him every time she saw him parade before a race that was televised; it was worse when he began to win and she watched another lad lead him round the winner's enclosure; watched the ceremony with the doughnut, which the crowd loved. Khazan and his doughnut were a constant source of jokes. He looked for it at the end of every race and every workout.

He was an idiotic horse and Debbie adored him. Bob teased her about the horse.

'Other girls are hooked on pop idols,' he said. 'Trust you to go overboard for a horse. Where do I come in?'

Debbie laughed.

'There's no comparison,' she said, and left Bob wondering exactly what she did mean.

'You shouldn't have asked,' Nancy said, amused by her son's expression.

'Don't get too attached to horses, Debbie,' Sally said. She had come down again, unable to appease the restlessness in her. 'They make a poor substitute for people.'

She hadn't realised how true it was. She turned her head

and saw Nancy looking at her thoughtfully, and went hastily outside to drive over to Jack who was an uncritical companion, delighting in her company. Nancy saw too much.

Debbie sometimes felt she lived in a kind of limbo, waiting for life to begin. School was now something to endure. The petty restrictions and regulations irritated her. She needed to be away from authority, to make her own decisions, to lead her own life. She looked absurd in school uniform, feeling like a grown-up dressed in her small sister's clothes. She shared very little of the other girls' world. Her own revolved around Jack and Les and the horses, around Sam and the flower farm, where she was now a great help to him, able to share the workload, see to the orders, make out the invoices, and work on the books.

'I'm staying here,' she said one morning, during the Christmas holidays. 'I can take over a lot of your work; and there's nothing I want to do, except be with horses. I can be with them here. Sally says we can have all their invalids and pensioners; and the money they pay is very useful.'

Sam looked at her and smiled. It was something he had always hoped for, but he wasn't going to push her. He didn't know that Debbie went off by herself later that morning to the beach, and stared for a long time at the chill grey sea and the bleak rocks, feeling she had signed away her future. She thought of Khazan, wishing desperately he could come back to her. She missed the show-jumping, and the excitement of riding him. There were other horses, but never one like him. He would come again at the end of April, she would spend all her time with him, renewing her pleasure in him and again there would be that dreadful break.

There was nothing she could do about that. She began to wish he would lose a race; and perhaps injure himself, not badly, but badly enough to come home to her.

And she knew it was stupid. She had to learn to grow up, but growing up appeared to be a constantly more difficult process. She had once thought that being adult meant the end of all problems, all difficulties, all shyness, but growing up just brought more and more problems and it was no easier to solve them than when she was small. And she wouldn't ask Sam; he had his own worries. Business was good, but prices rose all the time and profits didn't keep pace; they were always economising, always glad of every penny, always doing their own repairs to save the cost of labour. Jack was older and could not do so much, and Nancy, with the best will in the world, was hampered by living in a wheelchair, and sometimes irritated and frustrated, because she wanted to live a normal life, and there was never any chance of that.

Sally came less often after Christmas too. The weather was bad, and she had other pressures on her. Matt was totally absorbed by Khazan, sure he would win the Grand National, appearing briefly for meals, during which he barely spoke, but worked out training routines and diets, and if he did speak, spoke only of horses.

It was time to make big changes.

Sally began to plan. She could no longer drift on, as a background to Matt, finding her only occupation in her mares. She did not tell Matt what she had in mind. Better to wait till after the Grand National, and break it to him then.

She did not know how to carry out her plans and went to see a solicitor. He listened to her, his face grave.

'It's a very big step,' he said. 'Are you quite sure? Once you've embarked on this, it will be too late to change your mind. All the rest of your life is at stake.'

'I'm sure,' Sally said. She had lain awake, night after night, trying to make up her mind. Things could no longer go on as they were. She wasn't living. She needed a new start, a fresh way of life; to be important to someone; and that someone would never be Matt.

She told no one of her plans, not even Nancy. She avoided Cornwall because Nancy might guess, and she didn't want to discuss her future; she had made up her mind and wouldn't be deterred. But she would wait until after Matt's big race. With luck, he would win and appease his ambition, and then he might agree to her terms without any difficulty.

There was one more race before the Gold Cup.

Debbie watched it, sitting beside Nancy, on a pouring wet day, with rain beating against the windows, glad for once that she wasn't at the course.

Khazan hated rain. He danced in front of the cameras,

pirouetting sideways, and once kicked up his hind legs irritably, almost as if he were trying to unseat Steve. Steve, looking straight into the camera, seemed to be grinning at them. He loved the horse.

Debbie felt suddenly and violently jealous.

They had all the fun and she had none of it, stuck away down here. If it hadn't been for her the horse would be dead.

She watched as the tape went up and then Khazan was out in front and that wasn't the way Steve usually raced. He was pushing the horse all the way, and the horse was leading by an absurd amount, flying away from the rest of the field. Usually Steve lay well back. Debbie worried about the change in procedure and then she realised Khazan had taken the law into his own hands. Steve wasn't pushing him. He could barely hold him. And she knew why. The rain beating down . . . Khazan wanted to get out of it and back to his own stable, in the warm, out of the wind and mud, and he was pelting for all he was worth, knowing he had to get to the winning post, and then he could relax and be cleaned up and given his doughnut and go home to a feed in his stable, out of the weather.

'Idiot horse,' she said, as they flashed past the post. Matt wouldn't be very pleased; he hadn't wanted the horse to win by so much. But it was a good omen for the future. And then Debbie knew she didn't want the horse to win. He would cease to be hers; he would be a crowd-puller; a winter hero, belonging to everyone and she didn't want to share him.

Sally gave the horse his reward, the cameras turned briefly on both of them.

Debbie watched, finding it odd to see them on the screen, when she knew both so well. Sally smiled into the camera, but Nancy thought she looked strained, and wished she knew what was bothering her. Sally had seemed remote when she came to visit, only able to discuss the most superficial topics, never relaxed or at ease as she had been at first.

They had all been changed by the horse, Nancy thought, watching Debbie's face. Bob was watching Debbie too.

It was Jack that night who put all their thoughts into words.

'Nothing seems quite right since Khazan went,' he observed to Sam, as they walked together to give the horses their last feed. 'The excitement has gone out of life since Matt took him. Debbie's brooding; and business isn't too good. He was a good luck charm.'

'That's daft,' Sam said, but wasn't sure he meant it. They all seemed to be existing in a vacuum; nothing to aim for or work for; no fun any more. The horse had been fun. He had enjoyed Debbie's success in the show ring, even if they were only small local shows. There had seemed to be a future for all of them, then.

He looked out of the window at the bleak sky. It seemed years since the sun had shone.

Sally's plans left her in a state of alternate excitement and anxiety; sometimes there was a feeling of panic and she wished, more and more, that she could take Nancy into her confidence. But Nancy might try and dissuade her, and she didn't want advice. Her mind was made up. What was right for others was wrong for her; it was her life and only she could decide how to live it. All the same, it was a very big step, and as the day of the Gold Cup race drew nearer, she wished she had told Matt before, and that the moment of revelation was over.

She had no idea how he would take it. They had long ceased to discuss anything but horses. She wondered increasingly how it was they had come to drift so far apart. Horses were all of Matt's life; and they were only half of hers.

She wrote to Debbie, asking her to come up for the Gold Cup race, as Debbie would be on holiday then. Everyone could come with her, if they wished, the house was big enough for an army. She wanted to fill it with people; not with Matt's friends, but with her own; with Michael and Nancy and Bob and Debbie, with Sam, with Jack Savage. Nancy couldn't go to the race, it would be too cold for her in a wheelchair; she could watch at home, and they could talk in the evening. It was time to take her friends into her confidence.

She would go down and fetch them herself, driving the

big estate car. It would help pass the waiting days, help to ease the moment when she told her plans to Matt because there would be others there to cushion the aftermath; to help her over the most difficult time of all. Maybe Debbie could stay over the holiday. She needed another woman to talk to. Especially as Matt was so engrossed with training Khazan; with riding him, jumping him, learning to know him, against the day they would both go to Aintree together and come home with that cherished first place. Matt had no fear of failure. Maybe Debbie could stay over for both races.

Debbie wrote back excitedly; she would love to come, and so would Bob. But Nancy preferred to stay at home, Michael needed her. Sally was aware of jealousy; there was Nancy who, although tied to a wheelchair, was indispensable, and here was she, rattling around almost unnoticed, part of the set-up, taken for granted, always there to listen, but no one ever listened to her.

Anger overwhelmed her so much she almost packed her bags and left at once, but she had promised Debbie. She had already promised and it was up to her to see that the girl enjoyed every moment; life in Cornwall must be very dull for an eighteen-year-old.

Debbie and Bob drove up together. Jack Savage, at the last moment, decided to come after all, as excited as they were at the prospect of a big race. Cheltenham had always been one of his favourites. It was a difficult course, uphill much of the way, and a test for any horse. It would certainly show what Khazan could do.

The house seethed with speculation. Debbie and Jack and Matt pored endlessly over the form of the other runners, and Debbie went out to the stables to be greeted by that absurd long tongue, and by Khazan pushing at her, trying to discover the doughnut he was sure she must have in her pocket.

'I do miss him,' she said to Phil, his lad, and Phil grinned. 'He's a terrific horse,' he said. 'There's not one to touch him, here. We're all hooked on him.'

And then, suddenly, they were there. Cheltenham, and a wind roaring across the ground, and a pathetic ghost sun pushing reluctantly through the towering cloud. Packed stands and milling people; noise and litter and laughter and the constant call of the odds, the commentators and the tick-tack men, and the dark gipsies with their side-whiskers, brilliant eyes and animated expressions, twice as alive as anybody else, standing at the rails watching.

The early races, and the horses running and the slow relentless movement of time. Steve was riding in the first race and again in the big race. His face was tense. He barely spoke before running; everybody respected his need for silence. He nodded briefly as he climbed aboard. His young horse ran well and came second. Everybody was delighted as it had been expected to trail in an inglorious seventh, having shown no sign of running well all season.

And then Phil was leading Khazan, and Debbie was wishing she were there with him. As they came into the saddling ring, she went to the horse and patted his neck. He nosed her pocket. She had the doughnut.

'Afterwards, Mutt,' she said, and watched him trot off, prancing as he left the ring, breaking into a canter, pirouetting, that long tail swishing, his head turning to watch for the applause he was now certain was his due wherever he went.

The commentary over the Tannoy was recounting Khazan's story; how he had been shipwrecked, and rescued and recovered from near death, of his two names, of his two lives and his recent success. He was now a folk hero, gaining a place in people's hearts. They loved his demand for his doughnut and little Mop watching him by the winning post. Half the nation had put money on him, and a vast audience at home wished him well; and the bookies had brought his price down to evens; and his name was spoken, over and over, in a buzz all round the course.

They were off.

The commentator's voice was already excited.

'Khazan on the rails; can this horse do it?'

Debbie was holding her breath. The horses were over the first fence and already a faller, but it wasn't Khazan. It was an Irish horse. The horse was up and over, running free, leading the other horses. The riderless horse ran on, keeping with the pack, jumping when they jumped, flying to the front because it carried no weight. At the third fence it bumped into another horse and that made two fallers, and another free runner, but Khazan was up and over, too, and she was watching every minute, yet wishing she wasn't there, as a horse went down at the fifth fence. Her throat was tight and she repeated the old tag given to jumpers everywhere; throw your heart over and then follow it. She was holding on to Bob's hand without even knowing it.

She was watching the horses again as they came into sight, flying down the field, hooves thundering, jockeys crouched like monkeys on their backs. Khazan was lying third, meeting the fences right, jumping cleanly and well, landing perfectly, gathering himself to run on, and on, and up and over. The fences looked huge and the horses had to run uphill all the way with the wind in their faces, manes and tails streaming, and mud flying.

Khazan must not fall. He mustn't fall.

It was a litany, repeated over and over, a talisman of words.

They were out of sight and there were only the voices telling her what was happening. Debbie was out there with them, feeling every movement of the horse, knowing so well how he would meet each fence, eyeing it, collecting himself to rise and go over it as if he had wings on his hooves; if only he wasn't bumped; if only he didn't slip; if only ...

They were coming towards her again and she watched them, whispering 'Blaze, Blaze, Blaze.'

And once more she couldn't see anything.

The voice of the commentator was the only link with the race.

'Khazan has fallen. Khazan is a faller ...'

Debbie felt sick.

The voice began again and she could cheerfully have killed the commentator.

'No, it isn't Khazan. It's Deputy Sheriff. The colours are very similar. Khazan is against the rails, he's fighting it out with Honeydew Dancer; it's Honeydew Dancer from Glory Boy and Khazan and Merry Imp. Honeydew Dancer as they come towards me, it's Honeydew Dancer, giving way now to Glory Boy. Glory Boy coming up on the rails and it's Khazan, and Merry Imp, and Honeydew Dancer, a long way in front of the rest of the field, those four fighting it out now, as they come to the next fence.'

She couldn't look. She couldn't listen. She couldn't bear it. She was back in time with a horse dragging itself up the steps from the beach; a weary horse; an exhausted horse . . .

And then she had to come back to reality and the voices around her, and the yelling crowd, and the horses thundering over the ground, not so many now, some of them fallen, some pulled up.

The crowd's yells almost drowned the sound. She was standing closer to the rails and she could see the horses. Bob had pulled her but she didn't remember going; didn't remember anything as the runners came into sight at the last fence and the horses were piling at it and over it, and there they were and the announcer was jumping up and down and crazily shouting, beside himself with excitement, and there was Khazan, pounding along, close to the first few horses, the other horses masking her view for the moment. Blaze, Blaze, Blaze, Debbie whispered, forgetting his real name, forgetting everything, her fists clenched, the words choking in her throat. She wanted him to win and she didn't want him to, but he mustn't fall, he mustn't fall, he mustn't fall.

The announcer's voice was rising, he was spilling out the words, faster and faster, beside himself with excitement, and she ought to be shouting for Khazan, but she was clutching Mop, unaware that she had picked him up to prevent him from being trampled by the people pressing behind. She was immobilised, standing against the rails, unable to take her eyes off the runners. The voice was in her head, the words beating against her, and there was a hush as everyone listened or tried to see, and then more yells.

'They're neck and neck, all four of them, Khazan on the rails, beside him Merry Imp; there isn't a pin to put between Honeydew Dancer and Glory Boy. It's Glory Boy in the lead, with Honeydew Dancer falling behind. Khazan second and Merry Imp third, and straight down the line to the winning post.' The voice was cantering, never pausing for a breath, rising higher and higher with excitement.

'Khazan and Merry Imp are going ahead, neck and neck, leaving the other two horses standing, it's Khazan and

Merry Imp from Honeydew Dancer and Glory Boy. Can Steve do it, with his horse that came from the sea?'

A pause and the voice was away again, striving to keep up with the horses.

'It's Khazan; it has to be Khazan the winner, from Merry Imp. Khazan is lengths away and Merry Imp can never catch him now; no, it's still a race between these two; Khazan is losing ground; he's failing; he's limping, he can't keep up the speed; Steve's easing him off . . . is he pulling him up. They're only a few strides away from the winning post and it's Merry Imp making ground, Merry Imp's making all the running, Khazan just behind. It's Merry Imp, Merry Imp accelerating towards the finishing line, nothing else within miles of them; Steve's pulling Khazan up, walking the last few feet, and Khazan is second, trying to forge ahead . . . '

It was all over. They were standing beside Khazan while the vet examined him. Phil, silent, removed the saddle and put the rug over the horse. Steve stood anxious, wondering if he should have pulled Khazan up earlier; Matt watched the man who eased the leg in his hand, felt the leg, watched the horse move, up and down, limping badly.

'It was that last fence,' Steve said. 'He landed badly, but he was all out, trying to catch Merry. I'd have broken his heart if I had stopped him.'

Debbie knew it was true.

Khazan dropped his tongue into her hand as she stood beside him. Sally was watching Matt. There was no chance now of running Khazan in three weeks' time; that leg would not be right; and the Grand National course would finish him.

'Pulled tendon,' the vet said. 'He won't race again for a long time. It's a pity. He's a great fellow.'

Debbie found it hard to remember the rest of the day. Khazan pushed her. She had forgotten his doughnut. They had a second place to celebrate but somehow all the pleasure was gone; she watched the horse limp to his box. She hadn't wanted him to win, and now felt, superstitiously, that she had wished injury upon him.

Matt felt all his dreams had crashed around him. There was no end to the bad luck.

Debbie worried all the way back to Sally and Matt's farm. Only last night Matt had said he would have to cut some of his losses; get rid of a couple of losers; persuade the owners to sell them and buy something better. It was a hard tough world, like all competitive worlds, and there was no room in it for sentiment. Debbie knew then she wanted no part of it.

They ate almost in silence. There seemed nothing much to say. Bob watched Debbie and Sally watched Matt and Jack Savage thought of other times and other bad luck; and quite suddenly and irrelevantly of Chesterton's poem about Fleet Street, and quoted it, startling them all, as he spoke of all the truth they talk in hell and all the lies they write.

Matt lifted his head.

'They'll say I overworked him; gave him too hard a season,' he said.

Jack nodded.

'They'll say so,' he answered. 'They don't matter. We know the truth. It was bad luck; without that particular jump he'd have sailed home. He landed badly, but he was trying to avoid a loose horse; he hadn't a chance. It wasn't your fault; it wasn't Steve's fault; it was the luck of the game. We all did our best, no one can do more.'

It was some consolation but for all that Matt wondered: had he raced the horse too hard? Steve wondered: should he have pulled up earlier? Phil wondered: had he let the horse go too far or too fast in his training in the weeks before? Debbie wondered if the old injury had caused this bit of trouble; Khazan had been battered about in the sea; perhaps she should never have ridden him, but let him live out his days unknown and unnoticed.

It was so easy to be wise by hindsight. So easy to judge and condemn. For the first time, she found she needed Bob; needed him badly. She looked across at him. He nodded, and they went outside to visit Khazan in his stable. Jack Savage glanced at Matt and Sally, and went too, to talk to the lads who were doing the horses.

Sally said nothing. Sally had eaten nothing. She had played with her food. She wondered if her own plans were doomed. She should have told Matt before, but she had wanted to tell him when he was elated by winning; not when he was defeated by failure and the knowledge that this horse, his all-time beauty, might never win the race he had dreamed about for so long.

'Matt,' she said.

'I was so sure,' Matt said. 'I never thought of this. I should have known. Doesn't do to count your chickens.'

Sally looked at him. He had done it before. They still had one of the most expensive nurseries in the country. She went to her bureau. It was now or never. She couldn't wait until Matt had another winner. She couldn't go on living an empty life. She took out a letter and handed it to him.

'What's this?' he asked, looking at her stupidly, his mind still full of the chances he had missed; of the knowledge that he had a first-class horse and that that horse might be ruined forever; that he might never have so good a horse again, or another chance to fulfil a dream.

He glanced down at the letter, and then his attention was held.

His expression changed completely.

'Why wait till now to tell me?' he asked.

'You were taken up with Khazan. I wanted to tell you after the National; I thought we'd have our winner then,' she said.

Matt read the letter again.

'How old is he?'

'Three weeks old. He's with a foster mother; I've seen him four times. He's dark, like you. You can see him whenever you like. He can come home when he's six weeks old; that will be the day after Aintree.'

'What are we going to call him?' Matt asked. It was what he had wanted, almost more than he had wanted to win the National; a son to work with him, a boy to rear, to teach to ride; to teach about the horses.

'I hope he'll like horses,' Matt said.

'His father was a jockey. He was killed last autumn. His mother died when he was born. She rode too. It's in his blood,' Sally said. 'I didn't just want any child. I went to our solicitor, who started to search for me, for the right child. I was going to help his mother; perhaps half adopt the child, to come and stay with us. But as it turned out . . .

She named him for us. His name's Christopher Matthew.'

'Let's go and tell Debbie and Bob,' Matt said.

He had forgotten his disappointment; he was already planning, glancing across the fields, thinking of the pony he would buy next year and then school himself so that it was a gentle ride for a toddler.

Sally followed him. The house would no longer be empty. Soon there would be a noisy boy running from room to room; playing with Shiekh, asking for a dog of his own, a horse of his own. Matt turned and smiled at her, and she was glad that she had changed her mind.

Outside Debbie and Bob were talking to Khazan while Phil attended to his leg.

'We're adopting a baby,' Sally said.

'Can I be godmother?' Debbie asked, not knowing quite what to say to such a statement.

'You can,' Matt said.

'You deserve to be,' Sally said. 'If you hadn't been fond of Khazan . . . and come to stay . . . I might never have changed my mind. It's a lonely house when Matt's busy; and I can't live with the mares all the time.'

'You won't sell Khazan?' Debbie asked.

Matt looked at her; their life had changed so much and all through her. He thought of the two years of patience that had gone into making the horse fit again; and the life Debbie was leading just now, without her own horse; he knew that Khazan had been as much of a passion for her as he had been for him.

'I'm getting rid of him,' Matt said. 'He's earned his keep; and I don't think, even if he were fit, that I'd try him at Aintree; not after that breakdown today. It's been tough on him. Jack was right; I asked too much of the horse.'

Debbie said nothing. Khazan was to go, and she would never see him again.

Sally spoke quickly.

'Matt, don't tease. It isn't fair; it means too much to Debbie.'

'I'm sorry,' Matt said. 'I wasn't teasing. I thought Debbie would know.'

She turned to him, her eyes alight with excitement.

'He's coming back to me?' she said.

'He's going home,' Matt corrected.

Debbie kissed him, and kissed Bob, and put her arms around her horse. She couldn't show her face. She couldn't believe her luck. Khazan huffed and shoved her, wanting his evening feed. Mop, wandering round the yard, came to Debbie and wagged his tail.

She knelt to stroke him.

She would have them both.

'Perhaps you'll be happy to stay in Cornwall now,' Bob said, knowing that before she had only agreed to stay because of her father and his need for her.

She turned to him, and looked at him; there might be far more waiting for her than she had ever dreamed.

She raced to the house to ring Nancy and tell her all the news.

Bob stood at the stile, watching the horse, with his own plans for Debbie's future, in a few years' time. Matt and Sally stood together, talking about a mare, making plans for the pony that Christopher would ride, and Matt said, confidently, suddenly aware of a future, and of all the time in the world:

'One day, Christopher will ride our winner; we'll have that horse yet.'

Sally looked at the stable, and at Khazan's head watching them over the half door.

'We may have him now,' she said. 'Debbie got him right once. Perhaps she can do it again. You never know.'

'Red Rum did it, and he had leg trouble. Khazan might do it yet; but if he wins he'll win for Debbie, not for me. I'm transferring the horse to her,' Matt said. 'I have a future now. What are you smiling at?'

'There are several things I like about you,' Sally said, but she refused to explain what they were.

That night, nobody slept for hours. They were all dreaming dreams of the future, of a child growing up; of a wonder horse; and of a new partnership. Khazan dozed, unaware of human hopes and fears and ambitions.

In Cornwall Sam stood at the edge of the cliffs, watching the surging sea, knowing that Debbie would have all she wanted, and would be staying with him because she wished, and not because she felt she must. He looked down at the twisting steps and thought of the day, so long ago, when it had all begun, and of the horse lying there, almost dead, on the beach, and the long, slow struggle.

It had been a new beginning for all of them.

And now the road twisted again, and they were at yet another beginning. He did not even wonder how it would turn out; there was peace in the night, and all his doubts were stilled. Life had a purpose, even though sometimes it was hard to see. He had recovered his faith, but in a good world, not one run by a tyrannical deity he had invented for himself, out of misery.

And all because of a horse. Sam laughed at himself, and went to bed.

THE END